CARISSA'S
LAW

MISTY BOYD

CARISSA'S
LAW

MISTY BOYD

DEFIANCE PRESS
& PUBLISHING

Carissa's Law

ISBN-13: 978-1-948035-01-9 (Hard Cover)
ISBN-13: 978-1-948035-10-1 (Paperback)
ISBN-13: 978-1-948035-00-2 (eBook)

Library of Congress Control Number: 2018932284

Published by Defiance Press & Publishing, LLC

Printed in the United States of America

Editing by Janet Musick
Cover designed by Nathaniel Dasco
Interior designed by Deborah Stocco

Distributed by Midpoint Trade Books

Bulk orders of this book may be obtained by contacting Defiance Press & Publishing at **www.defiancepress.com** or Midpoint Trade Books at **www.midpointtrade.com**

Publicity Contact: www.defiancepress.com OR (713) 429-4366

*This book is dedicated to my parents,
my brother, my husband, and all those
throughout my life who believed in me.*

CHAPTER 1

C arissa Schultz pulled into the parking lot at the front of the huge university campus in Houston with what she hoped was plenty of time to make it to her 8:00 a.m. class. Still, she sat for a couple of minutes, wondering what her future held. What would it be like to change hundreds of years of ignorance about people like her? What would it take to change minds and hearts? Could she even do it? Was she strong enough? Well, today was the beginning of what she knew could be a momentous journey.

Finding her class was step one and she needed to make it on time. A glance at the schedule laying on the console reminded her of the room number. "College Algebra, Room 163, here I come!" She'd googled the campus layout the night before, and knew that Room 163 was in the math/science building.

If her pre-law degree hadn't required it, she would have steered away from algebra but, if math was necessary to meet her goals, she would tackle it, just like every other problem in her life so far. She'd seen her share of obstacles in her first eighteen years. Because of ADA laws, she knew the campus would be easily accessible, though she wondered if she'd have trouble finding the ramps that went from the parking lot to the buildings.

She grabbed the lightweight wheelchair from the passenger seat, pulled it over the top of her, and placed it on the ground outside her car. Snagging her backpack out of the back seat, she tossed it over the handlebars, then slid over into the seat.

She used this chair in her everyday life; it had been custom-built for her and was as comfortable as a wheelchair could be. It was manual and, because it was a hot, humid day, it might be a tough push. That's all I need, she thought, to arrive damp and sweaty for my first impression on the university world. Oh, well, minor problem.

She pasted a big smile on her face. "Change the world," she murmured. "Change the world, one quadratic equation at a time."

When she reached the math/science building, she pushed up the ramp and, as she rolled through the university hallways in search of her death room… ahem… classroom, she felt the familiar heat of all eyes on the girl in the chair. She should be used to it by now. It happened everywhere she went. Carissa, The Live Show, showing all times, day and night, for your viewing pleasure. Free, for a smile. Double price if you make a racecar joke.

There it was—Room 163—the Doom Room. She was a bit early, but that gave her time to settle into the new surroundings.

Rounding the corner, she spotted the most dreamy guy she had ever laid eyes on. Ever. Brown hair, brown eyes, chocolate skin, short but stocky. Definitely able to lift her… ahem… or other things, if needed.

She realized she'd stalled in the doorway like some kind of idiot, and he was looking right at her.

"Hi," he said, peering up from his notebook. "Looking for Algebra?"

"Uh… yeah, Algebra. Looks like I made it."

She rolled in, moving across the room from him to take a spot near the back. "Oh, my God, Carissa," she thought, "you have no chill. You see a cute boy and can't remember how your face works. How are you going to change the world?"

She did a quick survey of the classroom. Whiteboards covered three of the light gray walls. A short wooden lectern sat squarely on a long white table at the front of the room. The classroom chairs were silver metal with black plastic seats, lined up in neat rows of six at more of the same long tables. The rest of the class filed in, taking seats randomly. Her classmates were an eclectic mix of boys and girls: a couple of white kids, a trio of Hispanics, several blacks—including the cute guy she saw when she entered the room—an Asian couple and a girl from a Middle Eastern country. Some wore nice jeans and polos; a couple of the girls and one boy wore khaki shorts with tee shirts, and one guy wore bright, rumpled pajamas, looking like he'd just rolled out of bed.

The professor entered the room, wearing a harried frown and toting an oversized briefcase. He strode to the table with the lectern, ignoring the students, and set the briefcase to the right of the lectern. He was a short chubby man with steel-rimmed glasses, and what was left of his salt-and-pepper hair was pasted to his head as perspiration poured off his red face and down into a sparse black beard. Plopping a notebook on the lectern, he peered at the class over the top of his spectacles.

"Answer when I call your name," he ordered, his voice gravelly, as if he smoked a lot of cigarettes. Opening the notebook, he read a list of names, making checkmarks on a page as students responded.

Next, he reached into the briefcase and pulled out a thick paperback book. He held it up. "If you haven't already purchased this book for my class, pick it up at the Student Union bookstore by tomorrow." He turned and wrote the name of the book and the author on the whiteboard directly behind him. "And here's your assignment for tomorrow's class." He wrote a chapter number and a page range under the other information, then began the lecture abruptly. Kids started taking notes.

Before long, the lecture started to sound to Carissa like it was coming directly out of a scene in a Charlie Brown special. *Wah waaah, wah wah wahh, wah wah. X? Y?* Carissa had never understood why the alphabet had decided to get into a long-term relationship with numbers. The whole thing seemed doomed to fail. After what seemed an interminable amount of time, the professor ended the torture session and she was free to go.

Gathering her books, she could see the boy who'd welcomed her before class collecting his notes and shoving them into a backpack. He caught her gaze and smiled, revealing white, even teeth. He walked over to her. "Hey, rough hour, huh? Could that guy be any more draining?"

"Yeah, it was pretty boring. I don't think I could have sat here another minute, even if I could get up," she laughed. She was relieved when he didn't look at her like she was some sort of alien with two heads. Most people did when she joked about her disability, but she couldn't help it. It was part of her, a part she was comfortable joking about. It was the world that was uncomfortable.

"Great sense of humor," he grinned. "Are you headed to another class, or..."

"Oh, no, I'm done for the day. I figured math was enough torture for Mondays and Wednesdays. I torture myself with English on Tuesdays and Thursdays."

"Well, I was gonna get some coffee and go over the lecture in the food court. You wanna study?"

What? Dude, I can't even remember my name right now. "Carissa," she blurted.

"Um… what?" He frowned.

"My name is Carissa."

He held out his hand. "Oh. I'm Isaac. I probably should have said that sooner. So… study?"

She gave his hand a firm shake. "Yeah, sure," she said.

They made their way to the food court, wending through the crowded tables to the coffee bar, and the stares came again. *Boy, if she thought rolling solo was a magnet for looks, this dreamboat wasn't helping things at ALL.*

She grabbed a coffee and, before she could make her way to the cash register, he had paid for it and bought her a chocolate chip muffin. So much for the Miss Independence pants she thought she had put on today.

"Thanks. You didn't have to…"

He gave her another one of his contagious grins. "Oh, a beautiful girl should always have a nutritious breakfast. It's important."

She glanced up at him. She couldn't tell if he was joking or serious.

He seemed to sense her discomfort. "What's your major?" he asked, changing the subject.

"Pre-law," she answered. Whew, something she could talk about without turning eight shades of tomato. "I want to change things for people with disabilities, help make things easier on the next generation. So many people have the wrong idea about living with a disability. I want to change minds. I mean, it may not happen in my generation, but I'd like to know I did what I could. My life is good; it's different, but it's good. I want people to understand my life is worth it, and so are the lives of others like me."

"Wow, big goals. Well, I'm pre-med. My mom was injured in an accident right after I was born. I was in the car, but was uninjured. She ended up with a T-6 spinal cord injury. She never walked again, but it didn't stop her from raising me. She's my inspiration for becoming a doctor. I want to go into physical rehab. She thinks I'm crazy. She's not wrong."

"Looks like I'm not the only one with big goals."

Before long, they had discussed everything under the sun, including her spina bifida, and he hadn't flinched. Maybe this college thing would be okay.

CHAPTER 2

C arissa went immediately to her room after getting home from school. She wanted to avoid her parents, at least for the time being. She didn't want to talk about Isaac. And they would know. Mom would know. Mom could always read her. She didn't have time for that right now. She had to figure Isaac out first. And she had to figure out College Algebra, too, because there had been no studying, only talking to Isaac. She settled in for a long, boring afternoon of Xs and Ys, and some whys.

Later, Carissa heard a knock on her bedroom door. "Carissa, dinner! Come eat, and tell us everything, girl."

Oh, boy. This should be fun. Everything. Um… maybe just the math things. Subtract the boy thing.

She made her way down the hallway, wondering how she would hide the Isaac thing until she was sure there was a thing. There was no need to talk about a thing if it wasn't a thing, right?

She took her seat at the table as her mom brought over the

mashed potatoes. Her dad sat across from her, and his direct gaze would make it hard not to tell him everything. Direct face line! Maybe she could hide behind her plate if she put it in front of her face just right. Who needed food? Her plate would be a shield now.

"So, kiddo, how was school?" her dad asked cheerfully. Jim Schultz always got right to the point, which made him a good car salesman. He was tall and broad, with striking blue eyes and silver hair. She'd probably contributed to the silver.

"Uh... great. Pass the potatoes?" she replied, reaching toward the bowl.

He passed the potatoes, and her mom brought over the star of the show, the meatloaf. Boy, Mom could cook a meatloaf.

Sarah Schultz was short, and she wore her glossy brown hair in a cropped, swept-back style. Carissa noticed mild signs of aging on her mother's face, frown lines on her forehead and laugh lines around her mouth.

"Looks amazing, Sarah," Jim told her, love in his eyes.

Those two gave Carissa hope. Married twenty-five years, still just as much in love as she'd always remembered. Not everyone made it this far. Carissa knew from watching her friends' parents split up that her parents were a rare and beautiful breed. She was blessed to have them.

"Say the blessing, hon?" Sarah said. Her mom kept the dinner table a place to pray and share the day as a family.

"Uh, sure," Carissa responded. "Dear Heavenly Father, we thank You for all our blessings. We ask that You continue to bless us as we do our best to serve You and Your Kingdom, and love people as You love us. Please bless this food, and allow it to nourish our bodies, and bless Mom's hands for preparing it. Amen."

"Amen," Jim and Sarah chimed in.

Carissa scooped some potatoes onto her plate. The faster she could serve herself, the faster she could stuff her face and avoid saying anything about Isaac.

"So, how was math, Carissa?" Jim asked, filling his plate with food.

"It wasth mapth. It wasth hard," Carissa answered through a mouthful of meatloaf. If she strategically shoved meatloaf and potatoes into her mouth between questions, she could avoid talking about most anything. Surely that would work. And it did. Dinner was done, without a single mention of the thing that might not be a thing.

When she finished, Carissa took her plate to the sink and started back to her room, relieved.

Sarah called after her. "Carissa, don't forget that tomorrow you have your doctor appointment after class."

Oh, yeah. Her yearly urology testing. That was always a blast. At least with all the medical things she endured, this was one she knew well. She knew what to expect and how it would go and, most likely, she even knew what the results would say. "Neurogenic bladder, consistent with myelomeningocele spina bifida, level L1. No change since last year." Yep. She knew the drill, and she knew her body. This test was a piece of cake. It was the ones that might find something new that really scared her.

"Got it, Mom. I'll be there."

She continued down the hall to the bathroom to take all her meds and to do her nighttime medical routine. Besides being time-consuming and annoying, at least it kept her healthy. She was blessed to have been born in a time of such medical advances. Generations of people with spina bifida before had not had it so easy. Maybe that's what drove her... the thousands of people who had come before her to make her medical life easier, resulting in a longer life with less difficulty. It was her turn now.

She finished her routine and went to her room to catch some television before drifting off to sleep, thinking about Isaac, her future, and the future of those like her who might benefit from everything she had her heart set on. She didn't have it all figured out yet, but she felt a heart tug toward a career in government, making the world a better place for those with disabilities. She didn't know where it would lead, but she knew she was on a path to something great. She was just trusting God to pull all the details together.

CHAPTER 3

Tuesday morning began with the same irritating alarm clock bing as the day before, piercing Carissa's eardrums. Moaning, she rolled over to slam it off.

"Here we go," she mumbled, transferring from her bed to her chair.

She made her way to the kitchen, where she gulped a bottle of water for her kidneys and crammed a piece of toast in her mouth, before flying out the door for school. Secretly, she craved another chocolate chip muffin.

At school, she parked in the same spot as yesterday. Perhaps she was the only one using the handicapped spots. Could she be that lucky? One could hope. She lifted her chair out of the driver's side door, grabbed her bag, and set off to find her classroom. She had always been a skilled writer. English, no matter what level, should be a breeze.

Carissa found her classroom at the end of a long hallway in the

Humanities building. Another girl, chubby, with bright red hair and freckles, was already seated at one of about fifty chair-desks, wearing jeans and a white-and-red striped tee shirt.

"Hi," Carissa said.

"Hey," the girl replied.

"I'm Carissa." She extended her hand.

"Amy," her new classmate answered. "What's going on with your legs?"

Forward, wasn't she? Carissa was never quite sure how to respond in these situations. Car wreck? Spina bifida? Like she'd even know what that was... None of your business? It felt kind of intrusive. I mean, here was this stranger, and the first thing she wanted to know was the most personal thing about her. Sometimes Carissa wished her disability didn't stick out like a sore thumb. Maybe then people would get to know her, and not her chair.

"Uh... I was born with a hole in my spine," Carissa said. "My spinal cord was coming out of my back. It paralyzed me." There, that usually covered it. People didn't usually ask questions after the brutal, honest truth. She had been born with her spinal cord literally protruding in a bloody mass outside her back. Her mother had described it as a big, bloody bubble. Carissa had never seen it. There were no pictures. Her parents had been too traumatized in the moment to take any.

After everything they were told that day, Carissa didn't blame them. It was a miracle she had survived at all, according to her doctors. The doctor who delivered her explained that Carissa was paralyzed from the waist down, that she would never walk. She also would have bowel and bladder issues to go along with the paralysis and would need lifelong care for those. All this was if they could get a tube into her brain in time to relieve the crushing fluid—hydrocephalus was the medical term—that was sure to make her a "vegetable" if she lived through it at all. Yeah. She was blessed. She was alive. She was paralyzed, but she was alive. And life was good.

"Wow," Amy responded, not probing any further.

Carissa spotted a round table near the back of the room and, steering around the desks, she went over to it, moving a chair so she could pull her wheelchair up to the table.

English went as expected. She didn't expect any problems. This would be her easy class, her favorite class.

Just as she was getting into her car, planning a relaxed rest of the morning at home, she remembered the doctor appointment. Instead of going home, she made her way into the medical center, the teaching hospital where she had been a patient her whole life. She'd grab a bottle of water from the machine inside the hospital to drink before the test. They always wanted to be able to measure how much urine her bladder could hold before it exploded. And that was a guarantee. Her bladder always betrayed her on these days. It was a fight she couldn't win.

She arrived at the hospital in time to see an ambulance pull into the Emergency entrance, sirens blaring, and she whispered a quiet prayer for the person inside. She made her way up the handicapped ramp to the door and pushed the automatic opener. She took the familiar elevator to the third floor. Just outside the elevator, she arrived at the desk, gave the secretary her name and her doctor's name, and rolled to the other side of the waiting room.

"Crap." She had forgotten her water.

She went back to the desk. "Ma'am, do you think I have time to make a run to the vending machine before my test?" she asked.

"Sure. I'll tell them where you are if they come for you. Take your time."

"Great. Thanks."

She raced down the hallway to the vending machine and pushed the button for water. She really wanted a Coke, but she didn't want to explain that choice to her urologist. Water it would be. She chugged some as soon as the bottle came and secured it on her lap for the trip back to the waiting room.

Arriving back at the front desk, she saw a familiar nurse she'd known her whole life.

"Hey, DeeJae!"

A tall, slender woman wearing purple scrubs turned and flashed a big smile. Short blonde hair framed her sensitive face and hazel eyes sparkled behind rectangular glasses. "Hey, kid. You ready? Come on back." DeeJae motioned her toward the door.

"Ready as ever." Carissa followed DeeJae down the familiar hallway to urology. She'd made this trip more times than she could remember. She wondered why they didn't just name the hallway after her.

"We're here, kid. You know the drill. Cath into this cup, then get on the table. Everything off below the waist. Let me know if you need help. And I ran the student off. No guinea-piggin' for you today. Not my girl," DeeJae said.

"You're the best. I'll call you when I'm ready."

Carissa did as she was instructed. It was routine by now and, when she was on the table in the most vulnerable position possible, she called out to the nurse.

DeeJae made her way into the room and gloved up for the procedure. "Do you have the cup with your urine output?" she asked.

"Yeah, I put it on the table."

"Hmmm… not much today," DeeJae said. "Did you drink your water?"

"I forgot until last minute. I chugged, though, as soon as I remembered."

"Why am I not surprised that my favorite Coke-chugging patient didn't get her water today? Carissa, you know what I'm going to say. I'm not even going to bother. You already know." DeeJae gave her a warm smile to go with her pretend frown.

"I know. I know. I just don't like the taste. I'll do better; I promise." Carissa replied, half-feeling terrible for treating her body this way, and half-knowing next year wouldn't be any different. She knew water was best for her kidneys, but she just couldn't understand how people drank that stuff all the time. No flavor, boring, yucky water. Maybe she would try. Maybe.

"All right, I'm going to start inserting the tubes," DeeJae explained. "Let me know if anything hurts or feels different from the other times."

Carissa laid there as all the tubes and wires were pushed into all their various temporary homes on her body. It was uncomfortable, but paralysis did help. She could feel some of it, but was spared the pain she knew would have come had she had full sensation. She thanked God for that as another tube went in.

"Okay, I'm going to start the saline now. Let me know when you feel the urge to go."

After several seconds, Carissa thought she felt an urge of some sort, so she said so.

"Good," DeeJae said. "Now, let me know when you can definitely go to the bathroom."

After several more seconds, Carissa really had to go. She let DeeJae know.

"Great. Now tell me when you absolutely, positively cannot wait another second. You're gonna pee, RIGHT NOW."

It didn't take long. "I gotta go!" Carissa exclaimed, as she felt the familiar, "too late" warmth. "I'm sorry," she murmured. "I was too late. I had an accident."

15

"It's okay, Carissa. That's what we want to know. How much pressure can your bladder hold before it releases the tension? It's a little bit before you start yelling at me."

Carissa laughed. She loved DeeJae; she always knew how to make the best of a mortifying situation.

After getting cleaned up and dressed again, Carissa went back to the waiting room for her second appointment. The doctor would look at her tests, determine if there was anything of concern, and give her the results. Usually, after that, she was cleared for a year. This was the easy part. At least the probes were gone.

CHAPTER 4

D r. Taylor's office was freezing, as usual. This man and his sixty-degree tundra. She never remembered to bring a sweater. At least she had her pants on now.

She stared at the old familiar walls of the exam room for what seemed like forever. The tile floor was painted with rainbows. The same cartoon characters painted on the ceiling had been there since she was a small child. Several children's magazines and a toddler puzzle toy sat on a round wooden desk in the corner of the room. She guessed they were there to make kids more comfortable. She knew from experience that they didn't help.

Just when she thought she'd been abandoned and forgotten, the door squeaked open, and in came feeble, gray-haired Doctor Taylor. He walked hunched over, leaning on an elaborately carved wooden cane.

"Hey, Doc, how does it look in there?" she asked.

"Hi, Carissa," he said. "How have you been?" Without waiting

17

for her response, he continued. "I've looked at your test results, and I see some things I don't like. Are your parents here with you today?"

"Uh... no. I drove myself. Why? What's going on?" A shiver of fear ran through her.

"Well, I compared the results from this year's tests to those of last year, and I see some changes that may indicate a condition called tethered spinal cord syndrome. Have you heard of that?"

"No. What is it? Am I okay?" Now she was really scared.

The doctor leaned against the exam table, looking intently into Carissa's file. He ran his fingers through what was left of his hair. "Yes and no. I want to have you go in for further testing. Your urodynamic study shows some bladder changes that are indicative of changes in your overall spinal health, and I'd rather be cautious and have a look before things get worse," he told her. "We may be able to get on top of it."

"On top of it? What are you saying? It's going to get worse?"

He looked at her calmly. "It could, Carissa, but don't worry. We're going to look into it, and I'll do everything I can to make sure you get the best care possible. Don't worry. Let's make another appointment when your mom and dad can come in, and we can all talk together."

"Doctor Taylor, what does all this mean?" She could hear her voice starting to rise and tried to force herself to be calm. "Just tell me. I'm eighteen and I've dealt with spina bifida my whole life. I can take it. Just tell me what's wrong with me!"

"Okay," he said in calm voice, as if he hoped that would lessen her apprehension, "if you're sure you don't want your parents here. You are eighteen. Legally, you can take care of all this on your own, and you're a strong girl, one of my toughest patients." He paused, gazing at her thoughtfully. "Carissa, tethered cord syndrome is a condition in which the damaged part of your spinal cord is attaching and being pulled on by other structures inside your body, most likely, in your case, scar tissue from your original closure. What this means is there's a possibility of further bowel and bladder issues, and the loss of what little leg movement you still have intact. You would have a harder time transferring to and from your chair, and you may experience some severe pain if this is allowed to continue. Now, I'm not saying you have it, but your bladder is showing some definite warning signs, and I want to set you up for a MRI and a consult with a neurosurgeon here at the hospital."

"Neurosurgeon? Surgery? I need surgery again?" she blurted. She couldn't believe this was happening, had thought all the surgery was behind her. From the original back closure, to the various leg surgeries, and countless bowel and bladder operations, surgery had followed Carissa through her whole life. She just wanted to be done.

"Maybe, Carissa, maybe. I'm not sure yet. Let's just take a look and see what the MRI says."

"Okay…" she agreed, unconvinced.

* * *

Carissa sat in her car and cried for a long time. She couldn't do this again. Another surgery? She had already had thirteen surgeries. She felt like a human lab rat. Did this ever end? Was she ever just going to be stable? "God, please, I can't do this!" she cried out.

The drive home was long. She wished she had brought her

mother to the appointment with her. She had been going through an independent streak since turning eighteen three months ago, but maybe she wasn't so grown up after all.

She pulled up in the driveway and stopped. How was she going to tell her parents? They'd already been through so much with her. It seemed like she was constantly putting them through some new worry. She hated this for them as much as she hated it for herself. They didn't deserve this any more than she did.

But it was time. She couldn't sit here forever. She got out of the car and went inside.

Her mother was at the kitchen table, arms folded in front of her, fingers interlaced.

"Honey, Dr. Taylor called and told me. Are you okay?" It looked like she wouldn't have to break her mother's heart after all. Dr. Taylor had already done it.

"Mom, I don't think I can do this, not again. I can't let them cut me again! I'm so scared!"

"I know, honey. I know. But you're so strong. You're my girl. You can do this. God will carry you. And we don't even know for sure yet. Don't borrow trouble. I love you. We'll get through this." Sarah fidgeted in her chair, trying to convince herself to follow her own instruction. There was no need to panic about another operation until they had all the information. She knew that but, as she looked at her scared daughter, she could hardly hide her own fear.

"But, Mom, Kayla had surgery and never came off the table! What if…" Carissa had met Kayla at spina bifida camp when they were six. They had become fast friends, and had been attached at the wheels ever since. Kayla had gone in for a routine exploratory laparoscopy last year and had died during surgery. The autopsy revealed that Kayla had too much scar tissue in her abdomen, and one of the tools used during surgery had pierced a bit of intestine that was not where it was supposed to be, and intestinal fluid and acid leaked into her abdominal cavity. It ate at her organs before doctors found it, and she could not be saved.

"Honey, that will NOT happen to you," Sarah assured her. She got up from her seat at the table and went over to wrap her arms around Carissa. "There is no chance of that happening to you. They aren't even going into your stomach. It won't happen. You'll be fine."

"Okay, Mom. I just wish Kayla was still here. I miss her so much. I need her here with me."

"I know, baby. I know you miss her. She's here, though, in your heart, for always, until you see her again in Heaven."

When Jim got home that evening, before dinner was served, they gathered as a family to pray. Jim and Sarah laid their hands on Carissa's body and prayed against tethered cord syndrome, against surgery, against harm, and against further deterioration. They ended the prayer by giving the whole situation over to God. If Carissa had to have surgery, they would trust Him. He was their hope in everything, and He was in control.

Carissa loved when her parents prayed over her. There was nothing like it. It brought her such peace. When she went to bed that night, she was totally relaxed about whatever God decided.

CHAPTER 5

J im and Sarah laid in bed that night and talked about the day, about Carissa's doctor appointment and the news it brought.

"Jim, what are we going to do?" Sarah cried and spoke softly. "I wish I would have been at that appointment with her. She must have been so scared. I should have been there. Why didn't I insist on going? She tries to be so independent, and I try to let her, but she's still my little girl. She still needs me!"

Jim patted her hand. "Sarah, Carissa wouldn't have let you go to that appointment if you had tied yourself to her car. You know that. That child of ours is stubborn and independent because we made her that way. We had to! She will never survive without that stubborn grit, and you put it in her. Don't take it away now. She needs it. And she'll be fine if she needs surgery again. She's always fine. She's our girl. She doesn't know how to be any other way."

Sarah didn't know what she would do without Jim. He had been her rock ever since the day they learned about Carissa's diagnosis. He hadn't cried when he heard their baby girl might not make it. As soon as she could get out of bed, he had immediately taken Sarah down to the chapel and prayed and prayed. He took everything to God. That was probably why they had made it through everything so far. She loved him for it. She never had to worry long, knowing that her husband took everything to the Almighty.

"Okay," she whispered against his ear. "You're right. Let's get some sleep." Sarah fluffed her pillow and leaned into Jim's arm. He wrapped it around her and pulled her closer into his chest.

They kissed goodnight and, comforted, she fell fast asleep.

CHAPTER 6

Isaac woke up to his mom calling out to him from her bedroom. The caregiver must be late again.

"Coming, Ma!" He jumped out of bed and made his way into her bedroom, where he found her still in bed. Yep. No caregiver. Second time this week, and it was only Wednesday. It looked like he would miss class today.

He gently lifted his mom and carried her to the bathroom. He put her on the toilet to do her private things and told her, "Let me know when you're ready for the shower."

"Thanks, Isaac. Cindy's late again. I guess you see that. I hate that you have to do all this."

"Ma! You wiped my rear end for two years. I can help you out some. It's fine!" He left her to finish up and went to make himself some toast. He scarfed it down just in time to hear his name again and headed back to help his mom transfer to her shower chair.

He didn't mind any of it. She had raised him with all of her challenges, and it didn't bother him one bit to pay her back some. In fact, he saw it as an opportunity some people never get. It did look like he was going to miss Algebra, though, and that Carissa girl. He wondered what kind of impression he had made. Good? Bad? Creepy? He hadn't meant to come on so strong. There was just something about her. He had to know her. She was special. She was different, and not because of the chair. That was his normal. That wasn't different for him at all.

He heard his mom call out again. She was done showering and needed help transferring to her chair so she could go about her day. From what he could remember, she had a coffee date with her girlfriends. He helped her get dressed and into her chair. "Do you want some breakfast, Ma? You don't want to have coffee on an empty stomach. You know what it does to your bladder." Isaac had seen too many times the embarrassment that paralysis caused when his mother had too much coffee on an empty stomach. Her normal bladder spasms worsened and there was almost always an accident. He hated it for her, and did everything he could to make sure it didn't happen.

"I'll eat some eggs, but only because you're insisting. I don't know what I would do if I was out in public and had an accident. I know the girls would help me, but it's just so hard to take care of away from home."

Isaac was relieved his mom agreed, and he pulled out a frying pan, two eggs, and some butter. He began cooking, melting the butter, and then scrambling the eggs right in the pan.

Isaac looked at the clock. 9 a.m. He had already missed an hour of class, and an hour of Carissa. That girl. He'd been thinking about her ever since he met her, wishing he'd asked for her number or something. Anything. And now he wouldn't see her until Monday.

He finished the eggs and scraped them onto a plate. Walking them over to the table, he asked, "Ketchup?" His mother was the only one he knew who ate ketchup with her scrambled eggs. He didn't understand it but, if the lady wanted ketchup, he would provide.

"You know me. Don't bring those eggs to me without ketchup," she joked, but Isaac knew she wasn't kidding. He headed to the refrigerator for the ketchup, found it in the door, and walked back to place the plate and ketchup bottle in front of his mother.

"Here you go, Ma." He sat down across the table from her and watched as she poured an unreasonable amount of ketchup over the eggs. He crinkled his nose in her direction.

She scarfed the eggs down in record time. "There. I ate. Now I have to run. The ladies are waiting." She pushed back from the table, grabbed her purse, and headed out the door faster than Isaac could get out of his chair to open it for her.

CHAPTER 7

C arissa arrived at class early Wednesday. She was excited to see Isaac. She wasn't even trying to hide it. She had gotten up early, put on makeup, worn her best top, and made it to class in good time.

She rolled down the hallway like lightning and, zooming around the corner, she took her seat and waited. He would be here soon. But thirty minutes into class, he hadn't arrived. She wondered what had happened. Maybe she had been so weird he had dropped the class and signed up for an Algebra class across town. Yeah, that had to be it. She was always so weird around boys.

High school hadn't helped. She had dated some, but the boys she dated were always so strange about touching her, even holding her hand, like she was fragile or something. Like they might break her. She hated it! All she wanted was a real boyfriend who wasn't afraid to treat her like a real girlfriend. Instead, they were always so standoffish and skittish around her. She thought maybe Isaac would be different, but skipping class to avoid her sure pointed in another direction. Oh, well, same story, different prince.

The rest of class was boring and went mostly over her head. She had never been good at math. She didn't know how she would get through the rest of the semester. Day Two, and she was already drowning in a sea of letters and numbers that made no sense to her. She needed a miracle. Or maybe she didn't, if Dr. Taylor was right. Maybe she'd have to drop the whole semester. She hoped not, but it had happened before. She had missed most of sixth grade due to hospital stays. It was always a possibility.

"Don't borrow trouble," she reminded herself as she got in her car to go home.

At home, Carissa found her mother chopping what seemed like an entire garden into a giant pot. It smelled magnificent. She was pretty certain she smelled a yeasty aroma wafting through the air from a hidden loaf of fresh bread. "Smells good, Mom! What's cooking?"

"Stone soup!" Sarah answered, her back still turned to her vegetables and pot. Stone soup was another one of Carissa's favorites. It was potatoes (stones) and every other vegetable under the sun in a rich, flavorful tomato-based broth. At least that was Sarah's version. Carissa didn't know how anyone else did it, and she didn't care. Her mom's was the best version. She allowed it to simmer on the stove all day, and Carissa liked to come by periodically and "check the seasoning for her," basically just an excuse to dip a hunk of fresh bread in and get a taste before dinner. It was a tough job but, as they said, someone had to do it.

"Great! My soul could use some stone soup," Carissa said, unable to hide the crack of disappointment in not seeing Isaac today. She hoped Sarah was too distracted by the celery to hear it. Her mom stopped chopping and turned around. Guess not.

"Honey, are you still worried about what Dr. Taylor said? It's going to be okay. We discussed this. Give it to God, and don't borrow trouble. We still don't know."

Carissa shook her head. "No, Mom. I'm fine about that. It's nothing. It's probably nothing."

"What, baby, are you sick? Are you having symptoms of this tethered cord thing? If you're sick, I can call..."

"No. I'm not sick. It's math stuff. I'll be okay. Math is rough. That's all," she lied. She hated lying, but she knew she was being ridiculous about this boy she'd met one time. It's not like he had even hinted toward wanting more than a study partner, but he'd treated her differently. He saw her. He looked at her face, not her chair, and he wasn't afraid of her. For once, around a boy, she had felt just like Carissa. It was nice; it was easy. But she couldn't explain that to her mother. She wouldn't understand.

"Okay, hon, math stuff it is, even if it isn't. My only advice is to take it to God. He'll help you, and I'm still here if you want to talk about 'math' stuff. I love you. I'll call you for dinner."

That hadn't gone well. Her mother hadn't believed a word she said, but at least she got off her back pretty easily. That was one thing about her mom. She always knew, but she never pried.

Carissa went off to her room to study her math lesson and to stew about what she may have done to push Isaac away. One class was all he could stand with her. That must be some kind of record. At least the boys in high school didn't drop out when they met her; they just ignored her. Oh, well, moving on. Another one bites the dust.

She cracked open her math book, and the letters and numbers once again began to swirl in patterns she couldn't understand. She might as well have been trying to study a foreign language, except she had always been pretty successful with those. This language was completely alien. She didn't know how she'd ever get through it.

Two hours later, she found herself being startled awake by a knock on her bedroom door. "Carissa, dinner! It may not be good, though. Mom said she never once caught you checking her seasoning!"

Coming out of her deep sleep, she mumbled something that loosely resembled, "Coming, Dad!" and wiped the drool off her face. She made her way to the dinner table, still delirious from being awakened so suddenly. Math was the most boring topic ever. She didn't know how anyone stayed awake.

"Hey, kid! Mom says you're having math problems. Get it? Math... problems? Get it?" He gently slugged her in the arm, she guessed, to make sure she got the joke. "Math problems, Dad. Dad jokes? Really? Calm down." He was so cheesy, but she loved him. Other kids she knew didn't have dads like him. He was a special kind of cheese. Maybe a little stinky, but still good.

"Well, if you need help, I'm here. It's been a while since I took college classes, but I still have a good brain between these ears. You let me know."

"Got it, Dad."

Sarah put out the bowls for the soup, and Jim carried over the heavy pot and put it on the table. Jim blessed the food and, in no time, Carissa was dipping chunks of bread into a bowl of Heaven. She loved this stuff. It was good for a rough day of boys and Algebra.

In the middle of dinner, the house phone rang. Carissa was sure her parents were the only ones on the planet who still paid for a house phone. Soon, she thought, the phone company would have to cut it off, just to bring them into this century.

"I'll get it," Mom said, as she sprang up from the table. "Hello?

Yes. This is she. Yes. What? Hold on." She took the phone into the living room.

CHAPTER 8

After several minutes, Sarah came back to the dinner table and sat, replacing her napkin in her lap.

"Who was it?" Carissa asked.

"That was DeeJae, Dr. Taylor's nurse. She set up an appointment for a MRI on Friday, as well as a consult with Dr. Brock, the neurosurgeon there at the hospital, on Monday. I'm coming with you."

"Mom, you don't have to come. I'm eighteen. I'll be fine." But secretly Carissa was glad for her mother's insistence. No matter how grown up she tried to be, a girl could still be comforted by her mother. A mom hug could turn anything into something hopeful.

"I'm coming, and that's that." Sarah picked up her spoon, putting an end to the discussion.

Carissa silently thanked God for the pushback. "Okay, Mom. If you must."

The rest of dinner passed with more casual conversation about

Jim's day at work and Sarah's hilarious picture hanging efforts in the living room. When everyone finished, Carissa took the soup bowls from the table to the sink and Jim cleared the table of everything else.

"Anybody up for a game of Monopoly?" Sarah asked. "Carissa's the banker. Gotta practice that Algebra!".

"Mom!"

"I'm in!" Jim replied.

They settled in for some good family competition, which usually resulted in Jim losing his good Christian values for a moment. Nothing too bad, but until you've heard your dad call your mom a slimy mashed potato face, have you really even played Monopoly? Carissa loved evenings like this.

"I'm the car!" Jim insisted, grabbing the car out of the box before anyone could protest. "And you're all getting run over tonight!"

Carissa and Sarah both rolled their eyes at him and picked out their game pieces from what was left. The money was dealt out and the game began, Jim insisting on going first, as usual. Nobody minded. Carissa and Sarah both knew it was all in good fun, and Jim was the only one who really cared about the outcome of the game anyway. For Carissa, just spending time with her parents was what it was all about.

When Jim finally won, as he inevitably did, Sarah packed up the game.

"Well, I'm going to bed," Carissa said as the last piece of the board game was stowed. "Early class in the morning. Goodnight!"

"Goodnight, Carissa," Sarah replied, picking up the game box and putting it back on the closet shelf with the rest of the games. "And, if you want to talk about that 'math' problem, or any other problem, we're here. You know that. Love you, kid!"

"I know, Mom. See you in the morning." Carissa went off to take her meds and do her nighttime routine. When her chores were completed, she stretched out on her bed and fell fast asleep.

CHAPTER 9

"So what do you think is going on with her? Do you think it's this tethered cord thing? She seems off," Sarah said to Jim as she fluffed the pillows on her side of the bed. "Something's up. I know my baby, and this ain't her."

"I don't know, hon. She seems okay to me, but women smell things on each other, or something." Jim emptied his pockets on the dresser top as he got ready for bed. "I've never understood how you can just know by looking at her that something's not right. I don't get it, but I trust you. If you say something's up, something's up. What do you think it is?"

Sarah walked into the bathroom, undressing as she went. She lifted her pink satin nightgown off the hook on the back of the door and slipped into it. "I dunno, Jim. It's just that, since she started college, she's been different. I hope it's not too much for her. Do you think we should have let her take a year off?" She paused while she brushed her teeth, then came back into the bedroom. "Is she ready for this? Higher level classes… all the social pressure? I just don't know. That's my baby in there. I just want to protect her."

"I'm sure she can handle college. She's handled everything she's been handed so far, and she always comes out on top. You've seen how strong she is." Jim took his turn in the bathroom, still talking through the open door. "Now we just have to trust that we've done our best with her. We've raised her to know she can come to us. We've raised her to know the Lord. We've raised a strong, independent woman. Now, she's flying. Even if we want to grab onto her wings, we can't protect her from everything. Whatever it is, she'll either come to us, or she'll handle it. Gotta trust her, Mama."

She heard the sound of water running as he brushed his teeth, and waited until she knew he could hear her again.

"I know. I can't protect her from everything, but something's wrong. A mom knows." Sarah was frustrated, and she didn't like it. She sat down on the edge of the bed, exasperated.

Jim slid into bed beside her, pulling her down into his embrace. "Get some sleep, Sarah. It'll work out. Carissa doesn't know any other way. She's built like her mama. Schultz tough."

"Goodnight, Jim. I love you."

"Love you, too."

CHAPTER 10

It was getting close to dinner time, and Isaac decided on ordering a pizza instead of cooking or asking his mom to cook anything. He grabbed his phone, and scrolled to the number already saved for times such as this. When the man on the other end answered, Isaac put in his regular order of a small supreme pizza for his mom and a small pepperoni for himself.

Cindy, the caregiver, had not shown up for the morning or night shift. Isaac planned to call the agency again in the morning and see if he couldn't arrange for another caregiver to start soon. While they waited on the delivery, he decided to discuss the ins and outs with his mom. He didn't understand why it was so hard to just show up to a job. It wasn't like taking care of his mom was difficult. She didn't even need any real medical care. It was mostly lifting. She was completely independent in most of her care. She did most things herself.

"Ma, I'm going to call in the morning to see if the agency has another nurse to send out. You remember last time we had such a hard time getting someone out here. If I have to, I'll just stay home until we find someone reliable. I'll call my teachers and see if I can get extensions on all my work."

"Honey, I don't want you to have to do that." She shifted in her chair. "I can manage until someone comes."

"You can't manage," he replied, leaning against the kitchen counter and shoving his hands into his pockets. "That's three hours you'd be here by yourself. What if you fell trying to transfer from your chair to… well, anywhere? You're not as steady as you used to be. You can't manage on your own. I have to know you're okay, and I won't leave you alone for that long. It's either me or a caregiver and, until we find a decent caregiver, you only have the one choice."

"Isaac, I don't want you to put your life on hold for me." She shifted again, and wrung her hands uncomfortably.

"Ma, we're in this together. This isn't my life or your life. It's our life. I'm going to do what I have to do to make sure you're taken care of," he insisted, his hands still shoved deep in his pockets.

The argument was put on hold by a ring of the doorbell. Dinner was here. Isaac stepped away from the counter and headed toward the door. The pizza guy was a short, rotund man with brown hair mostly covered by a "Dave's Pizza World" baseball cap. After a short exchange of words and money, Isaac came back to the table with the steaming pizza and set it down, taking the chair across from his mother. They ate in silence, neither of them wanting to admit that Isaac was right. His mother couldn't make it on her own. If Isaac couldn't find her a caregiver, his medical career might be over before it started. When they finished eating, Isaac cleared the table and put what was left of the pizza in the refrigerator.

"Let's get you ready for bed, Ma. Do you want a shower?" he

asked as he turned toward her and walked her direction.

"Yes, boy, I sure could use one." She grabbed her wheels and pushed off from the table, heading toward her bedroom. Isaac followed and helped her out of her chair onto her shower chair when she got to the bathroom connected to her room. She wrapped her arms around his neck as he bent down, and he easily lifted her from one chair to the other. He kept her dressed so she could have her privacy.

"Let me know if you need any help," he called out as he left her to herself. He closed the door behind him and sat on her bed to wait for her to finish.

When she had completed her bath, he heard her call out, and he went in with her polka dot nightgown held out in front of him so she could dress herself. "Sorry," he said, "I guess we both forgot to grab this on the way in here. I'll go so you can put it on. I'm right outside the door."

He left and took his place on the bed again, thinking of what she would do if he weren't around. Before long, his thoughts were interrupted by another call from the bathroom, and he went to get her. They repeated the same transfer process to get her back into her chair and she pushed herself to the bed. Once there, Isaac carefully lifted her into the unmade bed and covered her up. It was a process they had memorized. They had done it a million times, since Isaac had grown to be bigger than his mother was. It required no words anymore, just well-rehearsed movements. When she was tucked in, Isaac kissed her on the forehead.

"Goodnight, Ma. I'll call in the morning and see if the agency has a more reliable nurse for you, but I doubt they have anyone you haven't run off yet!"

"You hush, boy, before I run your crazy self off," she ordered. "Go to bed. I love you."

"Love you, too, Ma!"

He went to his room, feeling angry about how his mom and other disabled people were treated. It was a shame, and it wasn't fair, although his mom was fond of telling him life wasn't fair. Still, this was his mom, and she deserved better than this.

After he climbed into bed, his mind drifted back to Carissa. He put his arms under his head, staring toward the ceiling and wondering what it was about her. He hated not being able to see her today. He would have bought her a hundred chocolate chip muffins just to see her smile again. He had never fallen so hard for a girl, and it had only been one day! Maybe it was because she was so passionate. She knew what she wanted, and she was going after it.

Could that be it? He didn't know. But he knew he had to get back to that Algebra class. He couldn't wait until Monday. He knew that was the first time in his life he'd ever had that thought. Maybe he'd ask her out for more than a muffin. Maybe he'd ask her to marry him! This girl had him all shook up. Maybe he should just ask for her phone number and see whether she'd slap him. Yeah. "Calm down, Killer. She ain't gonna marry you. She doesn't even know your last name!" he told himself as he drifted to the place where dreams are made.

CHAPTER 11

C lass on Thursday went smoothly, as expected, and Friday morning Carissa slept late. It had been a long, hard week of firsts. College was a different animal than high school, and Carissa had her work cut out for her, mentally, physically, and emotionally.

She had her MRI today, and she was nervous. What would it say? Did she really have this tethered cord thing? Maybe she didn't. Maybe she had just had a bad bladder day. That was possible, right? She clung to the idea as if her life depended on it. She had to. She couldn't even wrap her head around dropping out of her first semester of college for spina bifida. She didn't want to let it have that power. She hated when it took over her life and kept her from moving forward.

She decided to stop thinking about the semester, and just take today for today. Sometimes, if she thought too far into the future, she got overwhelmed, and she couldn't be overwhelmed right now. It was time to leave for her MRI.

She went down the hall, meeting her mother halfway between her bedroom and the living room. "Hey, kiddo, I was coming to get you. You ready for this?"

"I'm as ready as I'm going to get," Carissa said as calmly as she could, then ended it on a positive note. "Let's do it!"

Sarah smiled down at her. "You nervous?"

"A little," Carissa admitted, taking the lead and heading to the front door.

Sarah picked up the car keys and followed. "Yeah, me, too. But God is in control. He's already waiting for you in the MRI machine, warming it up for you."

"Sure, Mom. God is warming up the MRI machine. Whatever you say." Man, her mom was weird sometimes.

The car ride was quiet. Carissa had too much on her mind to make small talk, and Sarah let her daughter have the silence she needed. Besides, there were prayers to be said.

They arrived at the hospital and went to the familiar check-in desk. The woman at the front checked Carissa in and told them to wait in the lobby. After what seemed like a lifetime, a lady with short brown hair and wearing pink scrubs came around the corner and called her name. It was time.

"I'll be back, Mom." The fight to be her own person was still strong in her. She could handle this. Her mom would be right out-side. How bad could it be? It was just pictures, just like an x-ray, she told herself.

"All right, if you're sure you don't need me," Sarah said.

Carissa could tell her mom secretly wanted to insist on coming with her, but she didn't. She followed the brown-haired woman down the hall to the MRI suite, where she was told to put on the tiniest, most revealing, thin gown on the planet, and hop up on a long, narrow table with a tube on the end. "I'm going in there?"

"Yes, ma'am." The woman handed her something with a smile. "Just put these earplugs in and hold this button. It gets kind of loud in there. You'll hear some banging and buzzing. Don't worry. That's all normal," she reassured Carissa. "The button is in case you need to come out for any reason. Push it, and I'll come running. Some people get nervous and need a breather. Don't hesitate to push it if you get scared or just need anything. I'll be in that little booth back there taking pictures." She pointed to a glass-walled enclosure to Carissa's left.

"Yes, ma'am. Thank you." Carissa laid down on the long, thin table, and the tech put a pillow under her head and another behind her knees for comfort.

"All right, Miss Schultz, I'll see you in about forty-five minutes. Don't forget your button."

Carissa felt her body moving into the narrow tube head first on the sliding platform. Once in, she understood the need for the button. The tube was so narrow that it was just inches from her face as she lay there, giving her an instant feeling of claustrophobia. "Forty-five minutes of this? Oh, boy. Don't push the button."

Carissa laid there for what seemed forever. It could have been hours. Days, even. She was stuck in a tube she barely fit in. This was definitely the least fun she'd had in a long while. She hoped this would be the only time for this test. She wasn't sure she'd voluntarily lie down for another one. "Don't push the button," she reminded herself.

The soothing voice came through the earphones again. "How you doing in there, Carissa? Just a few more minutes. You're doing great! I'm getting some wonderful pictures out here. Just keep still for me."

"I'm okay," Carissa lied as she reminded herself again not to push the button. A few minutes later, she felt movement. She was coming out of the tube. Thank God, it was over.

"You did great, Carissa!" The tech was standing next to her now, smiling. "I've had grown men push that button on me and come flying out of there like lightning. But you were fantastic. You ready to go back out to Mom?"

"Yes, ma'am." Carissa was certainly ready. Ready to be out of this room and to never come back. And maybe more than a little ready for some Mom TLC. Carissa transferred back into her chair and went to the room where she had left all her clothes to get dressed again.

Once Carissa was dressed and back out in the MRI room, the tech handed her a CD of her scan, telling her to make sure to bring it to her neurosurgeon when she saw him, then she escorted Carissa out to the lobby where her mom sat.

"Hey, kid!" Carissa saw relief in her mom's smile. "How'd it go? Did you rock it?"

Carissa smiled back, although she wasn't feeling that relieved. "It was a narrow tube. I felt like I was buried alive."

"Hey, you know who else was buried and got out? Jesus. He had you the whole time. He was never gonna let you get stuck in there." Sarah gave her daughter a huge hug.

"Yeah, I guess not." Carissa let her mom hold on for a minute because it made them both feel better.

After that, Sarah picked up her purse. "Ice cream for old times' sake?"

"Sure." Carissa was always up for ice cream, and the thought made her smile as she led the way out of the medical center.

After they got in the car and belted up, Sarah said, "Call your dad at work and tell him you're done and we'll be home after a dairy treat. Tell him I love him."

Carissa called her dad from her cell and told him all about the

MRI, and how fun it was. She was sure he could smell her sarcasm over the phone.

"Okay, kid," he said, his cheerful voice booming over the phone, "not too much ice cream. Tell your mom not to spoil her dinner, whatever she's cooking. Lord knows we'll die if I cook. Love you both! Be careful out there."

He always made her smile, and now was no exception. "Love you, too, Dad."

She hung up right as her mom pulled up to the local ice cream shop. "Are you getting sprinkles? I'm getting sprinkles. We deserve sprinkles." And it was decided. Mom said sprinkles, and so it would be.

Carissa got out of the car and they headed into the shop. They ordered ridiculous amounts of ice cream and sprinkles, exactly as Jim had instructed them not to do. What he didn't know wouldn't hurt him. They scarfed giant spoonfuls until they both thought they would pop.

When they were almost done, Sarah reached over and took Carissa's hand. "How are you feeling, Carissa? Ready for these results? Nervous?"

"A little nervous. I mean, that CD has the results. It says whether I need surgery or not. My future, at least my immediate future, is on that disc. It's hard to just have it in my purse and know it has all the answers. I want to know what's on it but, at the same time, I'm scared to death of what it says. I dunno. I guess I just want all of this to be behind me."

Sarah patted her hand, giving her a gentle smile. "I know, sweetie. And it will be. Soon, this will just be another time in the long list of times you've come and conquered. I have faith in you. I've seen what you can do. I have no doubt you'll be fine."

Carissa hoped so. They collected and threw away their ice

cream trash and hit the road toward home.

"Well, hello, ladies!" Jim said as they walked in the door. "Good ice cream? Good girl time? How are my girls?"

"We're good, Dad!" Carissa rolled over to give her dad a hug, while Sarah closed the door behind them.

"Fantastic! Hey, I was thinking, since you guys have had such a long day, why don't we just order pizza and pop in a movie for the night? Give the chef a break?"

"That would be great," Sarah answered.

Jim got on the phone to order the usual, large pepperoni and mushrooms, extra cheese. It was the only pizza they could all agree on. They munched, and laughed at some random Netflix movie Jim picked about a B-level super hero in Tokyo. He sure could pick 'em.

When the movie was over, Carissa did her nighttime routine, then crawled into bed and tried to give the MRI results over to God. She couldn't wait until church on Sunday. Maybe the pastor would preach on something that would help her relax about all of it. If God wanted to, He could even change the MRI results on the disc as it sat in her purse. He could do anything. Carissa just had to trust He knew what was best. He always had before. He'd never let her down.

CHAPTER 12

"I had fun tonight, Jim," Sarah told her husband as she changed into her nightgown. "I think that was what we all needed to get our minds off of everything. Thank you for ordering pizza. I truly didn't have the energy to cook anything. And that movie? A slug super hero in Tokyo? Sometimes I wonder about your life choices!"

Jim went through his nighttime routine, too, dropping the change from his pockets into the dish on the dresser and laying his wallet next to it before going into the bathroom to brush his teeth. "Hey, one of my life choices was you. I don't get it wrong ALL the time, do I?"

Sarah laughed, waiting until he'd finished to say, "Well, I am a good choice. You certainly made ONE good decision."

"You and Carissa. My two best decisions," he said, climbing into bed. "I think I'll keep you both."

She leaned over to give him a kiss. "You don't have a choice,

Jim. You signed on the line. You're stuck with me."

He returned her kiss, then switched off his lamp. "And I'd have it no other way. Good night, love."

"Goodnight, Jim."

* * *

Saturday was quiet around the Schultz home. Carissa slept in, so Jim and Sarah had the morning to themselves.

"Coffee, hon?" Sarah asked Jim as he greeted her in the kitchen, still in his flannel pajamas.

"I need it," he responded, stretching like a bear coming out of hibernation.

She poured coffee into his favorite mug and brought it to him, running her fingers through his silver hair as he took the first hot sip. Black. He'd taken it that way as long as she'd known him. They met freshman year of high school, and she had known her fate was sealed. He was the one, come what may. Neither of them could have known then, though, what would come. They'd waited until after college to get married, and they struggled with infertility for years in the beginning.

When Carissa made her appearance on that little stick in the bathroom, Jim and Sarah were over the moon. They were having a baby! Nothing else mattered. The pregnancy had gone perfectly. Sarah was a champ at being pregnant, once she finally managed to get that way. Hardly any morning sickness, but a craving for pickles and cheese dip like you've never seen. Together. She'd dip the whole pickle into the jar of cheese dip, take a bite, then dip again. Jim said it ruined the cheese dip, the way the pickle juice invaded the cheese, but if that's what the little growing peanut needed, that's what the little peanut got.

At the anatomy ultrasound, the one where they were to find out the sex of the baby, they discovered that Peanut would, in fact, be named Carissa. It was a fantastic day. They were ecstatic for their little girl. Only later did they find out the gender scan was the typical D Day, or Diagnosis Day, for most parents.

Carissa's spina bifida was small, and went unnoticed on the scan. It wasn't until her birth that they found out the challenges she might face. For Jim and Sarah, their only daughter's birthday would be D Day. It was the best and decidedly hardest day of their marriage up to that point.

The doctor came in and started spewing big words that spelled doom for their little six-pound princess, who was whisked away in emergency fashion just as soon as she entered the world. Jim and Sarah hadn't even gotten to hold her. Jim had been able to lay eyes on her for a moment before they took her, but Sarah hadn't seen her at all.

Jim could remember everything. He remembered Sarah lying there, exhausted from the birth, as the doctor spewed the words that would change their lives forever. "The infant has myelome-ningocele spina bifida, obvious hydrocephalus, and possible Chiari malformation. It will never walk, talk, or feed itself. It was a mistake to bring it into the world. I'm sorry. I wish we had caught this sooner. We could have done something."

"It? IT? That's my daughter. The INFANT is my daughter. Her name is Carissa. She is my little girl. She is not an 'it' and you will not call her that again," Jim shouted at the doctor. He couldn't help it. He had only seen her for a moment, but he was already in love, and this doctor was talking about her as if she were some kind of monster.

"I'm sorry," the doctor replied warily, stepping back from Jim. "It's just… if we had known… this didn't have to happen. We could have stopped the pregnancy. I'm just so sorry. Mr. Schultz, she's dying. The spina bifida alone will kill her. These babies don't live. If the spina bifida doesn't kill her, the hydrocephalus will. It's just a matter of time. The spina bifida will likely get infected and, even if it doesn't, the hydrocephalus… there's excess fluid on her brain. The brain is being crushed. I'm so sorry. I wish we had known to end this."

"END THIS? You mean abortion! We would never! You will not say that in front of my wife again! You will treat my daughter! You will do what you can to save her life and, if God sees fit, He can take her, but you will not speak of killing her again!" Jim paced around the room like a caged tiger, livid at what the doctor had implied. He could never kill his daughter. He didn't care what the doctors thought was wrong with her.

"Yes, sir. We'll do what we can. But you need to know…"

"I know! Now go treat my daughter!" Jim raised his hand in the air and pointed toward the door and, with that, the doctor left the new mom and dad alone.

The whole day exploded from the happiest day of their lives to the absolute scariest in just minutes. They couldn't have known in college that their fairy tale would turn this direction.

"Jim, what's he saying?" Sarah asked in her drugged haze.

"That doctor is spewing nonsense and calling Carissa 'It' like she's not even a person! That's what's going on!" Jim came to Sarah's side, trying to settle himself, but still shaken from everything the doctor had said. Hydro-what was it? "It's going to be okay. We're going to get her the best treatment available. If she doesn't live, it'll be because God took her, not because we didn't give it our all."

"Jim, what is spina bifida? Is that the word he used?" Sarah raised up on her elbows in bed.

"Yes. I don't know what it is. All I know is we're going to give her everything we have until we have no more to give. After that, we rely on God."

As soon as Sarah was able to get out of bed the next day, she and Jim went down to see their girl. They wanted to KNOW her, whatever time she had on Earth.

When they arrived in the NICU, they came upon a bruised, squishy, potato lump of baby, all wrapped in gauze, with tubes coming out of just about every place you could stick a tube, and then some places Sarah wasn't sure you were supposed to. Tears streamed down her face and she struggled to stand as she saw her baby in such a condition.

Jim saw her waver and reached out to grab her so she wouldn't fall. "Look how strong our girl is," he told her. "She's so brave and strong, and we have to be that way, too. She'll lead us." He tried to bring comfort to both his wife and himself, but inside he felt like Sarah looked. Scared, overwhelmed, broken, helpless.

A tall, thin black woman in black scrubs came from across the room, pulling on a pair of gloves. "Hi, I'm Denise, Carissa's nurse. I assume you're Mom and Dad?"

"Yes, ma'am," Jim answered, still holding tight to Sarah, who was crying softly.

"She's doing well, all things considered," said Denise, her voice soothing. "Her lesion looks good. No signs of infection, and we're closing it later today. Would you like to see it?"

Jim and Sarah were afraid, but they still wanted to know their girl. All of her. Even the scary parts.

Denise removed the gauze from Carissa's back, and Sarah began to weep uncontrollably. Here was the thing the doctors said was killing her baby, and now she understood. There was a hole about the size of a quarter, bleeding and spilling out things Sarah was sure were supposed to stay inside. She was devastated. She couldn't hold Carissa for fear of damaging her spine further. She couldn't comfort her. She could only look at this sweet bundle of hopes and dreams, and pray to God she could beat the odds. Sarah wasn't sure, looking at Carissa, that she could. She turned into Jim's arms, burying her face in the comfort of his warmth.

"Let's go to the chapel," Jim said.

The nurse told them she would call them when it was time for the surgery, so Sarah agreed to leave Carissa for a short time. She and Jim found the chapel close by, and they had prayed there, crying out and begging God to help for what seemed like a lifetime.

Before long, Jim's hospital pager signaled that it was time to come hand their baby girl off to the surgeon. That was the first time they trusted a surgeon with the life of their child. They had done it again and again and, if the tests from Friday showed what they might, they would do it again soon.

This morning, Sarah remembered how hard it had been to hand their baby over each time and how hard it would be now, even though Carissa wasn't a baby anymore.

"Jim, how do we do this every time? How? I don't want to let another surgeon cut my baby," she cried. "I don't want to hand my only child over and put her life into someone else's hands again. How do we do this?"

Jim hugged her tight, smoothing her hair. "I don't know, Sarah. We just do, I guess. And we trust God to grab her hand when we let go."

CHAPTER 13

C arissa came down the hallway, her hair a mess and sleep still clouding her face. "Hey, what's for breakfast?" At almost 11 a.m., brunch sounded more reasonable.

Her mom looked up with a smile. "Well, your dad and I had eggs and toast. You slept through it, but I can make more."

Carissa shook her head, heading for the coffee maker. "Oh, no, that's okay. Is there still coffee?"

"Yep. Still warm. I got you a cup down this morning. Have at it," Sarah laughed, knowing Carissa's love for coffee. "Get your go juice! Are you sure I can't make you something?"

"Nah, I gotta get to the library. Book report due soon. I'll grab something from a drive-thru."

Sarah got up to exchange the cup she'd left out earlier for a travel mug so Carissa could take her coffee to go. "Studying on a Saturday? You go, college girl!"

Carissa poured a splash of coffee into her mug, followed by

epic amounts of cream and sugar.

"You might want to run a comb through that hair before you get where you're going," Sarah said, pointing to Carissa's head.

As she grabbed the appropriately flavored brew, Carissa said, "Will do, Mom. Thanks."

With a quick goodbye to her parents, she headed out the door to the library.

At the library, she managed to snag the closest spot to the door. Not bad for a Saturday. She combed her hair quickly, finished what was left of her coffee, and got her chair out of the passenger seat and down on the concrete parking lot. Once settled, she rolled inside to spend a Saturday with her head in a book.

She couldn't have prepared herself for who she ran into just inside the door, though. Isaac. Mr. Runaway himself.

She was about to leave before he saw her, but he looked up from his computer behind the desk before she could. "Hey, Carissa," he said, "what brings you here?"

She decided to act cool, answering, "Um, studying. College. Remember college? You were there."

"Well, yeah. I'm still there. Can I help you find anything specific?" Before she could shake her head no, he went on, "I'm off in an hour. Do you want to grab lunch?"

Now she was confused. "Uh… why would you want to have lunch with me?" she asked bluntly.

"Are you okay?" It was his turn to look confused. "I'm getting a vibe here."

Carissa moved farther into the library toward him, but angled into the study area. "Yeah, I'm good. I just… I don't want to get into it. I just thought some things I shouldn't have. It's good."

What was his deal? Coffee after class, pull a no-show, then just jump right into lunch today, like nothing was weird? He'd practically run for the hills, and now everything was fine? Boys.

"Oh. Well, I don't know what you thought, or what happened, but I think I need a cheeseburger in an hour." He smiled at her uncertainly. "You're welcome to come along. I'll come find you when they let me out of here for the day. Cool?"

She nodded. "Uh... cool, I guess. I gotta get to work. Paper due."

Was that relief in his face? "Okay. Talk to you in a bit."

Carissa went to a computer desk nearby and set up for studying. She wondered what was up with Isaac. She could tell when a guy wanted to bolt, and she'd definitely thought she'd gotten that vibe when he didn't bother showing up to Algebra on Wednesday. She must have made a horrible first impression if he had dumped an entire class over one muffin. And now, lunch? Just like that? She did not understand boys. Not at all.

* * *

Just as she finished the opening paragraph of her English paper, she saw Isaac walk around the corner.

"Hey! You good for a break?" He came over with an easy smile and looked down at her. "I'm off for the day and ready when you are. I can find a magazine, though, if you're not at a good stopping point. I'm good either way." To prove his point, he plopped into the chair across from her.

Carissa closed the book in front of her. "Nah, I can go now."

He immediately popped up from the chair. "Great! I'm starved. There's this new burger place down the street I've wanted to try. That okay?"

"Yeah, fine." It took her a few minutes to get her stuff together.

They moved out the door to his Volvo V70. He opened the door for her to get in on the passenger side and took her chair to put it in the trunk. It was kind of nice that she didn't have to instruct him on what to do with it. He just knew.

He climbed in on the driver's side and started up the car. "Hey, what did I miss in Algebra on Wednesday?" he asked, slipping it into gear. "My mom's caregiver never showed, and I had to stay home and help her with her stuff."

Oh, no. Was that why... Oh, no. Carissa felt awful. Had he noticed the cold shoulder? And all because he was taking care of his mom? Wow. He took care of his mom, and she'd made up some elaborate story where he hated her. College was hard again.

"Uh... hello? You there? What did I miss?" Isaac was staring at her quizzically.

"Oh... just a bunch of letters dancing with a bunch of numbers. I'll let you read my notes." And I'll never let you know what an idiot I've been, she told herself.

They arrived at the burger place, which was interesting. It turned out to be one of those restaurants where you got a standard burger, and then there were toppings upon toppings you could choose from—anything from plain old American cheese and mayo, to mushrooms, jalapenos, bleu cheese, and pretty much everything else Carissa had ever heard of. They ordered, and he paid. Again. They filled their cups up with soda, and found a table to wait for their food to come out.

Isaac had gone with bacon, cheddar, and mayo. Carissa chose bleu cheese, mushrooms, and garlic spread. She wasn't sure what kind of garlic spread they were talking about, but she was never one to pass up garlic in any form. And it wasn't like she planned on kissing anybody, right?

The food came, and it was delicious. Carissa would have to tell her parents about this place. Or not, since she was here with Isaac, who did not yet exist. To them, at least.

"So, how's life?" Isaac asked before shoving a french fry into his mouth.

"Uh... good... ish. I had a doctor appointment that turned into more doctor appointments. And I have another appointment to-morrow." She struggled not to show how nervous she was or what all these appointments might mean.

She just wasn't sure he could handle all of her yet. She was still feeling him out. His mom did use a wheelchair, but that was his mom. Was he willing to have two ladies in his life like her? His mom wasn't a choice. Carissa was. And she wasn't sure he'd choose to hang around.

"Really? What's going on with you? Anything you want to talk about?" Isaac asked, seeming to know just what to say.

Her heart melted just a little. "Uh... well, just some stuff came up on a test I had. They want to look closer. A day in the life. I'm sure everything will turn out fine." And she hoped he'd change the subject because she wasn't sure either of them was ready yet to go into more detail, though she really wanted both of them to be. Her mind was wandering places it shouldn't. For goodness sake, she hadn't even told her parents about him.

"What did they find? I mean, if I'm not prying." He looked at her, his gaze sincere and interested. "I don't want to pry. I'm just curious. You know, the pre-med thing."

"Oh, just some spinal cord thing. I had an MRI. They're look-ing for tethering."

"I've heard of that." He took another bite and chewed it thoughtfully before going on. "It's where your spinal cord gets, like, stuck to you?"

"Yeah, something like that. They say I have symptoms. I'm not too worried," she lied. She just couldn't get into it yet. Not this soon. "Hey, so what about this math class? Are you getting everything? I'm so lost. I understand numbers. I understand letters. I don't understand why anyone ever put them together."

"No way. Whoever thought of putting numbers and letters together and making college kids take classes about it was a total jerk. I'm just hoping to survive." Isaac shoved three fries in his mouth at once.

"Yeah. It'll be a miracle if I make it through the semester." Carissa sipped her soda.

They finished their burgers, and headed back to the library. Isaac parked behind her car and went to get her wheelchair from the back. When he got back to her side of the car, rolling the wheelchair up to the door, he said, "Hey, uh… I was wondering, while I have you here, could… I… uh… maybe call you sometime? To study? Or maybe for another burger?"

"Sure!" She grinned, delighted. She enjoyed his company, so why not? They exchanged phone numbers, and Isaac asked her to call and update him after her appointment on Monday.

Carissa agreed, and they drove off, going their separate ways. On the way home, she decided she better tell her parents about him before she started having to sneak her phone around in the bathroom. She'd mention him over dinner tonight. That should be fun. Dad always insisted on meeting every boy she was ever interested in, and he had not approved of a single one yet.

Yeah, mentioning a boy should make for great dinner conversation. But she really liked Isaac, so she would.

CHAPTER 14

C arissa got home and went inside, put all her books in her room, and came out to see what her parents were up to. She was just headed into the kitchen when her phone vibrated in her pocket. It was Isaac. "Already?" she thought.

She pulled the phone out and read the message.

"Hey, it's Isaac! Just wanted to make sure you got home okay. Not trying to be a stalker or anything. LOL!"

She replied, "Ha! Yeah. Thanks for today. That burger was great! Gotta go, though; talking with parents!"

"Okay, see ya!"

Oh, man. She'd have to tell her parents quick. She smelled actual phone calls in her future. Those would be harder to play off as a girlfriend, not that she had too many of those.

Sarah said from the doorway, "Hey, kid! How was studying? Are you hungry?"

Carissa went into the kitchen, wondering if her mom had heard her phone go off. "Uh... it was... productive. No, I'm not hungry. I grabbed a burger. I'm good 'til dinner."

"Okay. Spaghetti and meatballs tonight. Sound good?" Sarah grabbed a water bottle from the black refrigerator that matched the rest of the appliances and sat down at the square glass-paned kitchen table where Carissa had parked herself.

"Sounds great! Are you gonna add mushrooms and olives? Please?" Carissa looked up at Sarah and playfully put her hands in a folded praying position as if to beg.

"You know they'll be there. I'd never forget your olives," Sarah replied, giggling.

"Yum, can't wait! Where's Dad?"

"He went up to the church with Pastor to help set up some things for tomorrow's service. He should be home in time to eat with us."

Hmmm... separate parents. Carissa wondered if taking them down individually might be easier. One against one at a time sounded much easier than one against two.

Pulling together some courage, she said, "Hey, Mom? Can we talk a minute?" She folded her arms in front of her, fidgeting in her chair.

"Sure, hon! What's up?" Sarah took a long sip of her water.

Well," Carissa started reluctantly, "you know I have college and everything."

"Yes... I've been keeping up," Sarah got up and opened the fridge door to take out a bottle of chocolate milk, handing it across the table to Carissa. "My grown-up girl is in college now."

"Well, I kind of met someone. Kind of a boy."

"Kind of a boy? Or totally a boy?" Sarah grinned.

"Ha, Mom!" Carissa stuck out her tongue at her mom. "Very funny. Totally a boy. He's nice. He's in my Algebra class."

"Okay. Tell me about this totally a boy."

"Well, like I said, he's in my Algebra class. He's nice. We had coffee in the food court on Monday after class. He paid." Carissa rattled off these things like a grocery list.

"So far a gentleman..." her mother interrupted.

"Yes. And he bought me a muffin. I didn't ask. He just got it. Oh, and he's pre-med." Yes. Definitely mention the doctor part. That'll help. Hopefully. Carissa was starting to regret her decision to have this conversation twice.

"A muffin, huh? And pre-med? He sounds great. But drop the bomb, Carissa," Sarah said. "Go ahead. Hit me. Is he just out of prison? Killed someone? He has seventeen cats! What's making you so nervous?"

"Uh... well... just... I mean, I don't even know if it'll matter." Carissa wasn't sure how to bring the subject up. Oh, well, might as well spit it out. "We've never talked about it, so I just don't know. I mean, you and Dad aren't... well... he's black."

"Black? That's it?" Sarah laughed with just a hint of relief. "That's the bomb? Are you sure he doesn't have seventeen cats? Because the look on your face says he has seventeen cats, not that he's black." She got serious. "Carissa, I don't care what color he is, and your father won't either. He'd better treat you better than those other boys, though. I'm not kidding. Buying a muffin is a great start, but you're our princess. He WILL treat you that way, black, purple, or pink with polka dots. He WILL treat you well. Or else."

"Okay, Mom. So far, so good. We're not even dating yet." Carissa held her hands up, palms out. "Calm down. We just exchanged phone numbers today. He works at the library."

"Okay," Sarah said. "You know your dad's gonna freak. You haven't done well in the boys' department. I'm not sure he's ready to take this ride again, but I'll try to help you. You have to tell him over dinner."

"I will. At least it's spaghetti and meatballs. Give him an extra meatball for me?"

"You got it, kid. Extra meatballs for Dad. I'll do what I can." Sarah gave Carissa one of her "trust me" winks.

Carissa was relieved to have at least one part of the Isaac conversation over with. Unfortunately, it was the easy part. Dad would be harder. He was tough on guys Carissa wanted to date. She knew his attitude was coming from a good place, but it sure was irritating to hope a boy could pass the dad test every time.

Jim strolled into the house, as expected, just as Sarah finished up the noodles for dinner. It was like he could smell it from the church. Right on time.

"Hey, hon, how did things go? You and Pastor Mark get things set up okay?" Sarah called out from the kitchen.

"Yeah, all set. I told him about Carissa, too. He's praying. Told me to have her come up for prayer tomorrow if she wanted to."

"Great!" Sarah replied, meeting him with a kiss as he walked into the kitchen.

They sat down at the table to eat and prayed. Carissa could swear she was getting eyeballs from her mother's side of the table. It was time. She cleared her throat and went for it.

"Hey, uh, Dad? I wanted to tell you something," she said, moving a meatball around on her plate. "Mom already knows. But… I kind of met this guy. He's really nice, Dad. We're not dating, though. He's just a new friend. But… I like him. I know your rule." She looked at him with a touch of nervousness. "He'll come over for dinner before it goes further than friendship, but he might call sometimes. I just wanted you to know."

"A boy? A really nice boy? Okay. He'd better be really nice.

You don't have a great track record, Carissa. That last one you brought home… well, he's gone, and that's good. So, tell me more about this guy," Jim said. "Does he have a name? Where did you meet him? Does he have some kind of life goal? Because my girl has life goals. I don't want anyone holding you back."

"His name is Isaac. He's black…"

"She was concerned about telling us that part," Sarah interrupted.

"Mom!" Carissa admonished, then continued. "He's in my Algebra class, and he's pre-med. His mother uses a wheelchair, so he's pretty comfortable around me. I feel like I can just be myself around him, and not a girl in a chair. I like this one, Dad. I think he's good."

"Okay, kid. He comes to dinner, though, before anything happens. I want eyeballs on him." Jim shoved a forkful of spaghetti into his mouth without breaking eye contact with Carissa.

"Okay. I'll invite him for one night this week." Her father's gaze said that was the only right answer.

"Good deal." He finally broke eye contact and continued his dinner.

After dinner, Carissa helped Sarah clean up the kitchen before going to her room. Whew, she was glad that was over with!

Before she fell asleep that night, her phone buzzed again.

"Hey, I just wanted to let you know," Isaac texted, "my mom and I are going to pray for you in church tomorrow. I don't know if you believe in that sort of thing, but we do. You're covered. Goodnight."

"Goodnight. And, yes, I believe," she texted back. "Thank you, Isaac," she replied, a wide smile on her face. He prayed and went to church? He prayed! And went to church! That would pass the dad test, she was sure.

CHAPTER 15

S unday mornings were always chaotic in the Schultz house. Getting three people out the door for a 9 a.m. service was never easy, and they almost never got everyone out the door on time. But, just like every week, and maybe even more so this week, they were determined to try. They all got out the door only ten minutes later than planned. It may have been a Schultz record. Carissa couldn't remember a time when they ever made it to the car when they said they would. They hopped onto the freeway, heading to church, Jim trying to make up time. He always managed to get them there on time. Was flying down the freeway a sin? Because they did it every Sunday morning.

They arrived at the building, hugged the door greeters, and found seats in the aisle so Carissa could stay in her chair and still be with the family. The music started, and the choir started to sing a song Carissa had never heard before. The lyrics were about healing, and the idea that, even if God chose not to heal, the singer would still choose to have hope in Him alone.

Carissa looked up and saw her dad with hands raised high to the Lord, tears streaming down his face. Carissa started to cry then, too. Even if it turned out she needed this surgery, she would still have hope in the Lord. She always had, and she always would. She had been through a lot, but He had always been there. She trusted Him.

They really could have gone home after that. The Holy Spirit had shown up in worship and given them everything they needed. But, of course, they stayed for the rest of the service. When the Holy Spirit is moving, you let Him move.

After church was over, they went out to lunch. They always did, every Sunday, to discuss what each person had gotten from church that day. They ordered family-style fajitas with extra onions.

"So, that song, huh?" Jim said between bites of meat-stuffed tortilla.

"Yeah. I couldn't even deal," Carissa responded, digging in. She was always hungry after church.

"I thought I was the only one," Sarah agreed. "I guess we know all we need to know. Trust in Him, even if we have to do this surgery, right?"

"Right," Jim and Carissa confirmed.

There wasn't much talking about church after that. There was a lot of fajita scarfing, but not much talking. There just wasn't much to say. They all had felt it. God had come, and told them to trust Him, and they would.

In the car, Sarah piped up, "Have you heard from this Isaac boy recently, Carissa?"

"Um, yeah. He texted last night. Said he and his mom were going to pray for me at church today." Way to slide it in there, Carissa! Surely that had to score some Dad points.

"Great! Did you invite him over yet?" Jim asked.

"No, not yet, Dad. We're just friends. I don't want him to have to face the Dad Inquisition! You'll run him off before I even know if he's interested."

"Carissa, he's asking his mom to pray for you at church. He's interested in something. Invite him over on Friday," Sarah insisted.

"Okay." And that was that. She would invite Isaac over for dinner on Friday. Now all she had to do was summon the courage to invite him. She'd ask him tomorrow after class. Maybe she could get another chocolate chip muffin date before her big appointment.

* * *

When they got home, Carissa went to her room for more studying, so Jim and Sarah had some alone time. Sarah led the way into the kitchen, where she made some iced tea.

Jim sat down at the table, staring out the window for a minute. "Sarah, what do you think about this Isaac boy? Carissa doesn't have the best record with bringing boys into this house. I'm not sure I'm ready for another round."

"Jim, he's pre-med. He seems like he has some serious plans for his future." Sarah dropped ice into two tall glasses, adding a slice of lemon to each one. "He's not like those undriven knuckleheads she's brought home before. Besides, his mother uses a wheelchair. There's so much Carissa won't have to explain. He just knows all of her ins and outs. You have to admit, that's easier. And he prayed for her surgery. What eighteen-year-old boy do you know that has the head on his shoulders to have a good relationship with the Lord?"

"Me," Jim said emphatically. "I had a good relationship with the Lord at eighteen."

Sarah set the glasses on the table and slid into the chair next to Jim. "I rest my case. Give this boy a chance. At least let me feed him a good meal. You have full authority to kick him out without dessert if he doesn't meet your expectations."

"Deal," Jim agreed, taking a huge drink of the tea.

CHAPTER 16

Isaac had texted Carissa a few times since seeing her at the library on Saturday. He couldn't help it. He knew there was some rule about, "Don't text a girl for three days, or she'll think you're desperate," or something. But he didn't care. He didn't want to run the risk of seeming uninterested.

He wanted her to know his intention was to sweep her off her feet. He wanted no questions left unanswered about that, so he threw all the rules out the window. He was interested. He would say so. She was far too important to play around with. He would ask her to go on a real date, not burgers, this Friday.

He felt the sweat bead up on his forehead just at the thought. He hadn't dated much, for fear that people wouldn't understand his mom and all that was involved with being her son, but he didn't worry about that with Carissa. He only worried that she was too special for him. And she was. He just hoped he could prove himself worthy of a chance.

He decided to go talk to his mom. She was a woman. She knew women. He went out of his room and found her on the couch watching the weather.

"Hey, Ma, can we talk?" he asked.

"Sure, baby. What's in that head of yours?" She shifted on the couch to face him and patted the seat beside her. "Come sit down. We have some time before church."

"Well, there's this girl, Carissa. I met her at school. You know... the one I asked you to pray for. She's... well... I think I like her a lot. She's different than other girls I've met. It's only been a few days, but I... look... a man just knows things. I like her." He sat up straight, hoping she would take him like the man he knew he was.

"Isaac, my baby, a man and in love with a girl! Tell me everything. What's she like? You know you better treat her right. I won't have a man child of mine treating a woman with anything less than perfect honor!" She pointed a finger toward him, a stern look on her face.

"I know, Ma." He gently grabbed her pointed finger out of the air and held her hand. "I won't be like my father. You had to be daddy to me, and I know from you how a woman is supposed to be treated, not like you were."

"That's my boy! You look like you have questions only a woman can answer. Shoot 'em at me." She laced her fingers with his and waited.

"Well... I mean, she's just special. I think she's been treated badly by boys before me. How do I show her I'm not them? I want to do this right for her. I want to be the different one." He pinched his pant leg between his fingers, bunching it up, then letting it go.

"Honey, her past pain is between her and God. Is she a believer? God can fix anything for those who believe. You just pray for her and be the man I know you can be. Show her who you are.

God will fix her heart." She reached up and touched his face with her hand, looking deep in his eyes. "Now hand me my purse. The best place to pray for her is in church, and we're running late!"

Isaac grabbed his mom's purse from the coffee table in front of them and handed it to her, then helped her into her wheelchair.

"Weather man said it's a hot one today! That's Houston!" She wheeled toward the door.

Isaac followed her out the door and they headed to church in the Volvo, the air conditioning on full blast to counteract the heat. Upon arriving, they found their pastor, a tall, dark black man in a black suit, standing at the door greeting everyone who walked in, as he always did.

"Hello, Isaac, Betty! Two of my favorites. Come on in!" He extended his hand to Isaac, and Isaac pulled him in for a hug.

"Pastor Henry, good to see you today!" Isaac let go of Henry and stood to the side to wait for his mom.

"Betty, come here and give me a hug," Isaac heard the pastor say as he embraced his mother.

When the greetings were exchanged, Isaac and his mother took their regular seats in a pew on the front row, Isaac helping his mother into the pew from her chair. The choir filed in just as Isaac and his mother got settled. They started with "Amazing Grace," and sang through "How Great Thou Art," and "It Is Well with My Soul," before Pastor Henry got up to preach the sermon.

Isaac loved Pastor Henry. He had practically been his father growing up, and he loved the way the man brought the word every Sunday and made it so relevant to his life. This sermon was no different. It spoke right to his soul, and he left the church filled with strength and boldness he knew could only come from God.

CHAPTER 17

I saac invited Carissa to the food court after math class on Monday. Once again, he bought her a coffee and a chocolate chip muffin. "I hope you like those. I didn't even think to ask, but who doesn't like chocolate chips, right?" he said with a grin.

"They're delicious. Thank you, Isaac." Carissa accepted the muffin graciously. "Anyone who doesn't like chocolate chips is defective, for sure," she replied, as she plucked a single chocolate chip out of the muffin and popped it in her mouth.

"Hey, uh..." He hesitated, looking nervous, which made her nervous. "So, what are you doing Friday night?"

Oh, no. Friday night. She had forgotten. She was supposed to invite him for dinner. "I... uh... see... I'm supposed to... Do you want to come over for dinner? It's kind of a rule... My dad wants to meet any guy I'm thinking of... uh... My mom is cooking."

Wow, Carissa! Just put it out there. Oh, man, she was not good at this.

Isaac looked surprised, and maybe a little relieved. "I'll be there. Gotta satisfy the dad. See you then. Oh, and call me tonight after your appointment. I want to know what's up."

"Will do!" And that was that. Isaac was coming to dinner Friday night to meet the parents. "Speaking of my appointment, I should get home. I have to be there at 2:00. Mom and Dad both want to come, so I have to be home when Dad gets there. He took a half-day off today. Thanks for the muffin!"

Isaac walked her to her car, and she headed home, more than a little apprehensive. Now she had to worry about her appointment and dinner on Friday. She arrived home about the same time Jim did. They met in the wide concrete driveway in front of the house.

"Hey, kid! You ready for this?" he asked.

Carissa thought her dad sounded a little gruff, and she wondered if he was more worried than he looked. "Ready as I'm gonna get." She tried to sound positive.

"Me, too." He gave her a long look. "Did you talk to that Isaac boy? Is he coming to dinner?"

"Yeah," Carissa said. "I talked to him, and he's coming." She paused, then added, "He wants me to call him after my appointment and let him know what happens. I told him I would."

"That's great," Jim told her. "I can't wait to meet him, give him the ol' Dad speech."

"Dad, please," Carissa pleaded. "He's nice. Please be nice back."

"I'll be nice, but he has to qualify. No boy takes my daughter out of my sight without passing the dinner test," Jim said adamantly.

"Dad…" Carissa started.

"Come on, kid. Your mom is waiting for us." Jim waited while Carissa maneuvered into the house.

Inside, Carissa went into the living room to wait for her parents to get ready. It took a few minutes but, when all of them met in the living room, they gathered around to pray.

"Dear Heavenly Father," Jim started, bowing his head, "we come to you today to ask protection, guidance, and wisdom for all of us. You've always provided for Carissa and protected her from harm, and we simply ask that You continue more of the same today as we get these test results. God, You know we don't want Carissa to have to endure another surgery, but we'll do as You guide and instruct, because we know You have her best interests at heart. We love You, and we know You love us more than we can fathom. We lift this day up to You and leave it in Your hands. In Jesus' name we ask these things. Amen." He raised his head.

"Amen," Carissa and Sarah chimed in.

"Okay, let's do this!" Jim said, and Carissa sensed he was trying to sound more enthusiastic than he felt. In truth, she was sure he was scared to death to watch his little girl go through this again.

They all piled into the car and drove to the city.

CHAPTER 18

D r. Brock's office was the same temperature as Dr. Taylor's—freezing. Jim, Sarah, and Carissa sat in the examination room after Carissa's vital signs were taken and then waited to meet the neurosurgeon. No one said anything. Jim didn't make Dad jokes, and Sarah offered no comforting advice. Carissa didn't want to be there at all. It seemed like the cool gray walls were crowding in on them, threatening to crush the family in a cube of indifference.

They had been waiting for what felt like a lifetime, and then a white-coated man strolled through the doorway. Dr. Brock was young, with blond hair and hazel eyes, and about six feet tall. "Hi!" he said. "Where's Carissa?"

Carissa adjusted in her chair and piped up. "You're looking for me," she responded.

"Great! And you two must be Mom and Dad. Good to meet you all. "He shook hands around the room, and then took the rolling chair nearest to the computer.

"I see here that your recent urodynamic study showed some bladder changes, and Dr. Taylor is concerned about tethered cord, so he sent you to me. Is that accurate?"

"Yes," Carissa answered.

"And you had the MRI I ordered for Friday?"

She nodded. "Yes."

"Great! Let me go get that file and take a look, and then we'll talk about what I see." He rose from the chair and shook everyone's hand again, starting with Carissa's. "Then we can come up with a plan."

"Okay," Carissa murmured.

Dr. Brock stepped out and left them alone again.

"He seems nice. Respectable," Jim said.

"Yeah. I like him," Sarah replied. "You're quiet, Carissa. Everything okay?"

"Just nervous," Carissa admitted.

"I know, baby. At least we'll know what we're facing soon. Hang in there." Sarah patted her daughter's knee.

Just then, Dr. Brock stepped back into the room. Carissa felt her heart speed up.

"Okay, so here's what I see," Dr. Brock stated. "The bladder test alone doesn't necessarily point straight to tethered cord, but that, along with what we see here on the MRI, is definitely cause for concern." He took his seat again and looked directly at Carissa. "Carissa, I had the opportunity to look over some of your past MRIs, ones you may not remember from being so young, and I do see some changes I don't like. There is definitely some new tethering going on and, based on the bladder changes, I think it's best we intervene now to prevent further damage. I would like to go in and take a look to see if I can move the spinal cord away from the structures it's stuck to right now. Hospital stay is about a week, depending on how well you do, and full recovery can take up to six months. You'll be able to resume normal activities long before that, though. It'll just be harder for a while, again, depending on how well you recover."

Carissa felt hot tears fill her eyes and drip down her cold face. She couldn't do this again! She hated spina bifida and all that came with it, especially being cut repeatedly. She hated everything about surgery, and this doctor wanted to do another one. She couldn't do it. She just couldn't. She looked over at her mom for comfort, and saw tears streaming down her face, too. "Mom, I can't do this again."

"Yes, you can, baby. You're stronger than you think. I've seen you come through so much worse. We'll do it again."

The room fell silent.

"I'll leave you guys alone to process all this," Dr. Brock interrupted the silence, "and I'll let my secretary know you need to schedule a pre-op. Take your time. Come out when you're ready, and we'll take care of the rest." He got up and leaned down to place a hand on Carissa's shoulder. "Carissa, I'm very good at what I do. You don't need to worry about that. I'll see you guys outside." And he left them alone.

They didn't talk much. Carissa cried. Sarah held her, and Jim held Sarah. They just sat there in silence for a long time, until Jim broke the silence. "Come on, guys. Let's go schedule this thing... show it we're not afraid."

They went down the hallway to the receptionist's desk, where Jim explained they needed a pre-op appointment for a tethered cord release.

The girl, a short, pretty brunette with dark eyes, looked through the notes on her desk. "Yes, sir. For Carissa, right? I've got the paperwork right here. Dr. Brock said he'd like to get her in as soon as possible, at least by the end of the month. We have pre-op appointments, typically on Mondays. How is Monday, a week from today?"

Carissa nodded. She would likely have to drop out of school for the semester. The way Dr. Brock was talking, recovery was all dependent on how her body took the surgery. There was no way to tell for sure when she'd be able to come back.

And what about Isaac? Would he stick around if she wasn't in his Algebra class anymore? She hoped he didn't lose interest. All of this was just terrible timing, and she hated it.

They finalized the appointment and headed toward home.

"Carissa? You okay?" Sarah asked from the front passenger seat.

Carissa took a breath. "Yeah, just absorbing. I guess I'll have to drop math and English this semester. I'll email my teachers when we get home. I just hate all of this. I was really getting somewhere, and then spina bifida showed up again. It seems like I go so long, and everything's fine, and then BAM! Hit by the spina bifida truck again. It just gets old."

Sarah nodded. "I know, but maybe this will be the last thing for a while. I hate it, too."

The rest of the car ride home was quiet, as each of them tried to grasp the weight of it all. They all had their own ways of coping and, for now, silence seemed the most soothing thing for all of them. They just sat. No radio, no conversation. Just each individual, lost in thought.

Carissa thought about what to tell Isaac. Could he handle this? Weeks of recovery, where she may not be herself at all, and definitely wouldn't be up for chocolate chip muffin dates. She hoped he would hang around. She really liked him.

When they got home, they went their separate ways, Sarah to

the kitchen, and Jim to his home office. Carissa went to her bedroom to email teachers and text Isaac.

Once the emails were sent, Carissa felt empty. She was the kind of girl who needed to be doing something, accomplishing things, and now she was just stalled out, waiting on this surgery. She decided it was time to tell Isaac.

"Hey," she texted. "I just got home from the doctor."

He texted back immediately. "How'd it go?"

"Not great. They found what they were looking for. Pre-op is Monday."

His response came quickly. "Oh. I'm sorry. I don't know what to say. I didn't want this for you. Are you okay?"

She hesitated a moment, her fingers hovering, then began to type. "Uh… yes, and no. I just hate this. I have to drop my classes. There's just no way I could keep up."

"Oh, no," he exclaimed. "Does this mean no more chocolate chip muffin dates? I really liked those."

That made her smile. "Yeah. I guess so. I just can't imagine doing school and this surgery."

"Yeah, I get it. Hey, maybe I could just bring the muffins to you?"

"Well, that's fine. You can if you want to." Her dad would like that, because it would mean Isaac wasn't giving up.

"So are we still on for dinner Friday night? I understand if you're not up for it. No pressure."

"Oh, yeah, we're on. Recovery starts after surgery! I plan to just keep living until then."

"Great," he said, and she felt him grinning. "I'll see you Friday night."

Well, he was still on for dinner. That was good. She just hoped he could handle surgical recovery.

* * *

When they got home, Sarah retreated to the kitchen and the small table in the corner. Tears welled up in her eyes. How could she make her little girl lie down for another surgery? Every time she had to hand her daughter over to another surgeon, it broke her again. It made her feel like she had failed as a mom, not to be able to fix these things without putting her little girl through such agony. How could she do this to her again?

When she saw the tears streaming down Carissa's face in the doctor's office, it broke her heart. Carissa was such a strong girl. She had no idea. She'd been through so much in her short life that most people never even had to think about. Sarah knew she'd conquer this surgery, just like she had every other one, but that didn't change the hurt in her heart at seeing her daughter cry.

* * *

Jim was devastated. He wandered into his office, ignoring the files and boxes everywhere. He sank down in his desk chair and buried his head on his arms. He was a fixer, but he couldn't fix this, for either his daughter or his wife. Both were distraught at the thought of going through another operation and, if he was honest, he wanted to cry right along with them. He hated to see his girls hurt. And he hated not being able to pick up the pieces for them. Why did they have to go through this again? It wasn't fair, and he felt helpless.

CHAPTER 19

The next week went by about as fast as flowing molasses, but it was finally Friday. Carissa sprang up from her bed, using her arms to bounce over to her chair, her legs following, and rolled down the hall to ask what was for dinner.

"Hey, Mom! I was just wondering what you had planned for dinner tonight? Isaac is coming over."

"Did you think I would forget 'the boy' was coming for dinner?" Sarah gave her an indulgent look. "I was planning on chicken Alfredo. Is that okay? Does he like Alfredo? Is he allergic to anything?"

Carissa thought about it for a moment. "That's a lot of questions, Mom. I don't actually know what he likes, or if he's allergic to anything, but your Alfredo is the best. If he doesn't like it, he can't come back!"

"Okay, honey," Sarah said. "I'll stick with the plan, then. Make sure your chores are done before he gets here."

"Got it, Mom," Carissa called over her shoulder, going to her room to clean up and make her bed. Making a bed was the worst chore from a wheelchair. But she managed it, and now she needed a shower.

That would have to wait, though. The rest of the chores still beckoned. Before she knew it, it was lunch time, and she hadn't eaten a thing all day. She went to the kitchen to make a sandwich of sliced deli turkey, mayo, avocado, tomatoes, salt and pepper, and cheddar cheese before her last daily duty, loading the dishwasher. As she ate her epicurean delight, her mind drifted to what dinner might be like.

Had Mom convinced Dad to be nice? She hoped so. Would Isaac be nervous? She was certainly nervous. She hoped it wouldn't be so bad for him. She hoped her dad didn't run him off for good.

Carissa finished her sandwich and decided to do all her medical junk early today. She definitely didn't want to run Isaac off early or, even worse, leave him alone with her parents for an hour while she did all her personal things. She couldn't imagine what kind of torture her dad could manage to dish out in an hour of alone time with a boy his daughter liked. She didn't want to imagine it. She headed off to the bathroom for her pills and her nighttime routine to save Isaac from what, she was sure, would turn into the end of the world. He could not be left alone with her parents. She'd do anything to prevent it.

After she finished her bedtime routine and shower, it was time to start preparing dinner, so she went to the kitchen to help her mom. Sarah insisted on having a tablecloth for the table, and it was laying on the table waiting to be spread out. She told Carissa to set out the nice china plates and crystal glasses that had belonged to Carissa's grandmother.

Carissa collected the silverware, plates and glasses, and placed them on the table. After that, she helped cut up the chicken and season it, and measured out ingredients for the Alfredo sauce.

"You sure are helpful tonight," Sarah said with a smile as she put the ingredients into a saucepan.

"Uh… yeah…" Carissa said, "I dunno. I guess I just want to contribute."

"I think you really like this boy, and you have nervous hands," Sarah replied, stirring the sauce.

"I do. Do you think Dad will go easy on him?" Carissa asked.

"Of course not. But, if Isaac's everything you've said he is, I think everything will be fine."

"If you say so." Carissa sounded less than positive.

"I do say so, but you know your dad loves you and is going to grill every boy that comes in this house until you move out."

"I know," Carissa said, "I just wish…"

Just about then, Jim sauntered through the door. "Smells great, honey! Chicken Alfredo, my favorite. Are you trying to butter me up for this boy? Take down my guard?"

"Maybe a little," Sarah responded.

"It's working," he said, kissing her.

"You guys are so gross!" Carissa covered her eyes with both hands in mock horror. "Please don't do that in front of Isaac."

"I'll think about it," Jim replied.

"Dad!"

"Okay, okay." He gave Carissa a hug. "Maybe."

"Ugh."

Just then, there was a knock at the door. Carissa started to go answer it, but her dad stopped her.

"I've got this," he said.

"Daaaad!" she whined.

He lifted a hand to silence her. "I'll be nice."

"Nice," she thought. He might as well bring the shotgun, hounding him at the door first thing. Good grief.

CHAPTER 20

J im opened the door. "Hello, you must be Isaac," he said. "I'm Mr. Schultz, Carissa's dad. Come on in."

Isaac stood at the door, hands clasped in front of him. "Yes, sir," he said. "Nice to meet you, sir." He held out his hand, and Jim shook it. "I'm Isaac. Thank you for inviting me to dinner."

"It's our pleasure, Isaac," Jim said, standing aside to let Isaac in and herding him into the living room. "Have a seat. Dinner is just about ready."

Isaac sat gingerly on the edge of the couch. "Great. Thank you, Mr. Schultz. I'm starved. Can't wait!"

Carissa rolled into the living room.

"Hey, Carissa," Isaac said, getting to his feet.

"Hey!" Sorry about the dinner Nazi, she thought to herself.

Isaac was dressed nicely in a light blue button-down shirt and khaki pants, with brown dress shoes. He looked very presentable, Carissa thought. Almost too presentable to be eating dinner at her house. Her family usually ate in shorts. Her dad sometimes ate in his bathrobe.

Today, though, her dad looked pretty formal, and acted that way, too.

Jim picked up the conversation. "So tell me about yourself, Isaac. Carissa tells me you're pre-med. What brought that on? Have you always wanted to be a doctor?"

"Well, yes, sir," Isaac said, sitting down on the sofa again. "My mom was injured in an auto accident after I was born. She came out with a spinal cord injury and uses a wheelchair, so medical is kind of all I've ever known. I take care of her when her nurses don't show."

Jim looked impressed. "Wow. That's a lot to take on for an eighteen-year-old boy. Where's your dad?"

"What? Where's his dad?" Carissa thought. "Too personal, Dad. Too personal." Carissa didn't even know Isaac's last name, and her dad was asking him questions like she was about to take it.

"He hit the road shortly after my mom got hurt," Isaac answered with a shrug. "He couldn't handle it, so I don't really have a dad. But my pastor is always around to help out if I need a man to weigh in on things. He's kind of taken that role. He's there if I need him, so my mom and I make out okay."

"Well, it's wonderful that he steps in like that," Jim said. "Every boy needs a man to look up to."

"Yes, sir," Isaac agreed.

"Hey, guys, dinner is ready! Jim, why don't you come help me bring everything to the table?"

Mom to the rescue!

"I'm so sorry," Carissa told Isaac as Jim went to help Sarah. "He's like this. He's going to grill you all night. He's so overprotective. It drives me nuts."

"Hey, it's okay." Isaac followed Carissa into the dining room. "You're his daughter. I'd be the same way if some guy was coming around my baby girl. Good men don't mess around when it comes to their daughters. I don't blame him a bit. I respect that. He's not playing, and he wants to know I'm not playing, either. I'm not. Carissa, I really like you and, if this is what it takes to get close to you, I'm in."

Wow. Just wow. She had no response. No other guy had ever reacted that way to her dad and his torture. Most, she never heard from again after a night with him. She was really impressed with how Isaac was taking it.

He helped her get settled at the table, then took the seat next to her.

"Okay, who wants to pray?" Sarah asked, as she came around the corner with a big bowl of pasta.

"I'll do it," Isaac spoke up. "I mean, if you don't mind, Mr. Schultz. It's just, I'm the man at my house, so I'm used to being the one to do it. This is your house, though, so you make the rules, but I'd be honored."

"Well, then, go ahead, Isaac. We'd love to have you pray," Jim responded.

Carissa couldn't even breathe. Isaac was taking this all so well, and now he was praying over dinner? Who was he? Muffins? Prayers? Hanging in with Dad? Was he perfect? He couldn't be, but he sure looked good from where she was sitting.

Isaac prayed over their meal, and threw a little bit in there for Carissa's upcoming surgery.

Sarah started passing food around the table.

"This is delicious, Mrs. Schultz," Isaac said after his first bite. "Now I know why Carissa talks about your cooking so much. She's not wrong to brag on it!"

"Thank you, Isaac." Sarah seemed a little surprised by his comment. "I appreciate the compliment."

"So, Isaac," Jim leaned into the table, crossing his hands in front of him and Carissa cringed. "You and your mother live alone? What's that like? You're the man there, you say?"

"Well, yes, sir." Isaac put his fork down and straightened up in his chair, making solid eye contact with Jim. "Without my dad being around, I've had to step up some. My mom needs extra help, more than Carissa. She's a chair user, too, so when the caregiver doesn't show, I'm it. It hasn't been easy, but we manage." He loaded his fork with more pasta.

"And what does that look like for Carissa? How do you plan to make time for both her and your mother? Do you have time to devote to a relationship?" Jim shifted in his chair. Carissa wanted to melt underneath the table.

"Sir, your daughter is very important to me. I'm a man who makes time for what's important to me. Carissa won't be neglected. I promise you that." Isaac didn't flinch. He seemed unaffected by the frank questioning.

Jim wasn't finished. "How are your classes going? Do you get good grades? Carissa is a smart girl. She does well in school and works hard for her grades. I don't want that to change because a boy came around. This isn't high school anymore. Her grades dictate her future. A temporary boy doesn't need to get in the way of that." He took a long sip of his iced tea.

"Jim!" Sarah interrupted, dropping her fork against her plate, which made a loud clang.

"It's okay, Mrs. Schultz. Mr. Schultz, with all due respect, I don't date temporarily. I don't believe in wasting mine or any young woman's time like that. I don't know where Carissa and I are going, but my heart is not set on being temporary."

Carissa was sure she felt her heart stop beating.

"So, you plan to marry my daughter?" Jim had stopped eating altogether now.

"Well, sir, I can't answer that. What I can say is that I don't date to play games. She's special. I'm not wasting her time." Isaac now had his hands folded in his lap. He wasn't eating, either.

"I made cake!" Sarah pushed away from the table and went to the kitchen counter. She came back with a two-layer masterpiece, covered with chocolate frosting and a caramel drizzle.

"Looks delicious, Mrs. Schultz!" Isaac piped up.

"Thanks, Mom!" Carissa said, half-thanking her for the cake, half-thanking her for stopping the slaughter.

They ate, and Isaac and Carissa helped clear the table while Jim and Sarah went into the living room.

When they finished, Isaac said, "Hey, I'll be right back."

"Okay…"

* * *

Isaac went to the living room where he found Mr. and Mrs. Schultz.

"Mr. Schultz, can I have a moment of your time?" he asked.

"Sure, Isaac," Jim said. "What's up?"

"Well, see, I really like Carissa, and I respect you as her father. I was wondering if you would allow me to take her to a movie tonight, if she accepts, of course. But I wanted to ask your permission first. I know you only want the best for her, and I'd like a chance to show you I can be that."

"Isaac, you're one of the most outstanding young gentlemen

Carissa has brought home," Jim said. "In fact, you may be the only outstanding gentleman she's brought home. You can take her to a movie. Have her home immediately after, and respect her while you're out."

"I wouldn't do anything less, sir," Isaac promised. "I'll treat her the way I'd want my mama treated."

"Good deal." Jim beamed at Carissa's new boy.

"Mr. Schultz, I'll have her home immediately after the movie, and she'll be returned to you just as I found her," Isaac said.

"Drive carefully then," Jim told him. "That's my precious cargo you have there."

"Yes, sir. I understand. "Now, I just have to go see if she even wants to go out with me!"

"I have a feeling…" Jim replied. "I'll see you guys later."

And with that, Isaac went back in the kitchen to woo the girl.

Carissa looked up as he came back into the kitchen. "Hey! Where'd you go?"

"Oh, I was just squaring things up with your dad before I ask you out to a movie tonight." Isaac grinned. "He's cool with it, so the only one I have left to convince is you!"

"You asked my dad?" Carissa was astonished.

"Yes. You're his daughter before you're my anything. I felt it appropriate to ask him." Isaac strolled over to her, putting his hand on her shoulder. "Now, are you going to put me through all that for nothing, or are we going out?"

"Oh, we're going! You've earned it!" Carissa finished up what was left of the dishes, grabbed her purse, and off they went.

* * *

"Admit you were wrong to be so hard on the boy, Jim," Sarah said playfully.

"I might have been a little harsh…" Jim didn't look even a little sorry.

"Did you ask my dad for permission to take me on our first date?" Sarah asked. "I don't recall."

Jim glanced at her, smiling. "I'm not sure I did. Can we go back in time?"

"Nope. You were a scoundrel! No fixing it now," she teased. "He's a good guy, Jim. I like this one."

"I think I do, too."

CHAPTER 21

In the car, the conversation went smoothly. "I like your parents. They really love you. They don't play around with your heart or your safety, and I won't either." Isaac glanced over at her. "Put your seatbelt on. I want to bring you back to your daddy exactly like I found you."

"Okay. Hey, you know what? It just occurred to me that I'm going on a date with a boy, and I don't even know his last name," Carissa stated. "How irresponsible is that? Sir, I'm going to need to know your last name before this car moves an inch!"

"Why? You thinking of stealing it? Haha!" Then he said seriously, "It's Carter. Isaac Carter. I took my mama's last name when I got old enough. She raised me. She should share a name with me."

"Isaac Carter." Carissa smiled. "I like it. We can go now."

"Well, then, ma'am," Isaac laughed, "I'm glad we got that out of the way."

When they arrived at the theater, they approached the ticket counter. "Two for the new Star Wars, please," Isaac requested.

"Caregivers are free for the disabled. You don't have to pay, sir," said the attendant.

"I'm her boyfriend." Isaac told the attendant, and Carissa wondered how he had read her mind. "I need to pay."

"Oh. I'm sorry. I just assumed..." The attendant looked uncomfortable.

"Everybody does." Carissa answered her, with just enough sass in her voice to let the woman know she was not okay with it.

They took their tickets and headed toward the concession stand, where Isaac decided he wanted to get a popcorn and soda to share, after making sure that was okay with Carissa. "I can get you your own. I don't mind."

"No, this is fine. We can share. You don't look like you have cooties. Do you?" She peered up at him as if she were trying to determine if he was being truthful.

"Nah! Got my shot in first grade. I'm covered!"

"Good!" Carissa said with fake relief. "Then we can share."

"All right then. One large popcorn, and one large cola, please."

The snack attendant readied their order, and Isaac took both items, knowing from experience with his mother the struggle it was to push a wheelchair and hold things.

They went to find seats in the theater. Luckily, there were open spots in the handicapped section in the back. That wasn't always the case when Carissa went to see a movie. Sometimes she had to ask an able-bodied person to move so she could sit with her friends. They slid into the comfortable seats just in time for the lights to go dim and the previews to start.

Isaac wondered if it was too early to try to hold her hand, then he decided he didn't care. He was going for it. He reached out, gently put his hand on top of hers, but felt a bit of rejection when she pulled away.

"I'm sorry. I just... I rolled through something gross on the way in. My hand is sticky. I didn't want you to touch it. I think it's soda. I hope it's soda," she explained, embarrassed.

"We can take care of that. I thought you were rethinking the cooties thing!" He quickly grabbed the soda and a napkin, wiped some of the condensation onto the napkin, and took her hand in his to clean it off. When he was done, he kept her hand.

They sat through the entire movie like that, neither of them letting go of the other's hand. Passing the soda and popcorn around was a challenge, but they figured it out.

"Hey," Carissa nudged Isaac to get his attention. "I have to go to the bathroom. I'll be right back."

"Okay," he said, letting go of her hand and taking the popcorn from her lap.

She wheeled off, struggling to get the door to the theater open. Those things were always so heavy. She managed, being her stubborn, independent self, but admitted that maybe she should have asked for help.

She found the bathroom at the opposite end of the theater from where their movie played and went in. Inside, she found a familiar scene. All the stalls were unoccupied except the one reserved for wheelchair users. She tried to push into one of the regular stalls, thinking if she was careful she might be able to transfer to the toilet without the handrails that were standard in the stall built for people like her. No such luck though. Her wheelchair wouldn't fit and she had to wait. She sat, less than patient, with a full bladder. It seemed like she was there forever when her phone buzzed. It was Isaac texting.

"Are you okay? Did you find the bathroom okay?"

"Yes," she texted back.

"Are you sick? You've been gone a while. Chewy is about to start some mess in here! Might want to hurry back."

Carissa giggled to herself. "I'm okay. Someone is in the wheel-chair-accessible stall. I can't fit in the other ones. I have to wait."

"Ah. Gotcha. I'm sorry."

When the woman came out of the only stall Carissa could use, things were just as Carissa thought they might be. No wheelchair. No visible disability to speak of.

The woman looked embarrassed. "I'm sorry. I like to use this one because it's the last one. I figure it's cleaner because no one wants to walk down to it when all the others are available," she said, hanging her head and walking to the sinks.

"It's the only one I can use," Carissa said, hurrying to open the stall and get inside before her bladder erupted.

The woman finished washing and drying her hands without responding. Carissa finished her business and hurried to get back to Isaac and the movie.

When the movie was over, Isaac put Carissa's wheelchair in the back of his car, and they headed back to her place. He glanced over at her and took in how pretty she was, and how lucky for him that she was sitting here next to him. Should he kiss her when they got there? He wasn't sure. He'd told her dad he'd be respectful, but he didn't want to leave any doubt in Carissa's mind that he had had a good time with her. He wanted to do this again, and he wanted her to know that.

"Carissa, I had a good time tonight. All of it. Even being grilled by your dad was fun in its own way," he told her, trying to keep his eyes on the road, but stealing glances at her.

"Really? You enjoyed that assault, huh?" She looked over at him, a smile on her face.

"Hey, if my daughter was as pretty as you are, I'd be giving it to every guy who dared to look at her. I understand why he was like that." He took the right turn that led to her street.

"Did you really mean what you said about not dating for temporary?" She looked at the floorboard of the car, not wanting to make eye contact.

"I did. I don't date to mess with girls. This is not a game for me. I'm serious about you." He grabbed her face in his hand as he said it, gently pulling her up to look at him.

They pulled into the driveway. Isaac hopped out to get her chair out of the back and brought it over to her side of the car.

After she moved over to the chair, he asked, "Can I walk you up?"

"Sure," Carissa replied.

And so he did. He took the longest walk of his life up that driveway, contemplating whether or not to kiss her. When they got to the front door, he still hadn't decided.

"Look, Carissa," he said, "I had a really good time tonight, and I want to do it again." He paused for a moment, just gazing down at her seriously. "I want you to know that. And I also want you to know something else. I told your dad I'd be respectful, and I will be, but I want to kiss you goodnight, and I'd really like it if you'd let me."

She contemplated his solemn face for a second, then laughed. "You can kiss me," she responded, and Isaac knelt in front of her chair, put his hand gently on her face, and sweetly kissed her lips.

"Respect. I told your daddy I would respect you and, if I don't stop now, I might cross a line I don't mean to." He stood, then moved with her up to the door. "Let's go in."

Carissa smiled, opened the door, and found her parents waiting up in the living room.

"We're back!" she said.

Jim walked over to stand next to Carissa. "Did you guys have a good time?"

"Yes, sir," Isaac replied, "and she's home in one piece, just as you asked."

"Thank you, Isaac. I might even let you take my girl out again, if she'll allow it."

"I'd like that, sir." He shook Jim's hand, and gave a little bow to Sarah, who smiled up at him from the sofa.

"Goodnight, Carissa. Call me after your pre-op." And with that, he was out the door.

CHAPTER 22

The weekend flew by, probably because Carissa was dreading Monday so much. Now it was Sunday night. Her phone rang. "Hello?" she answered.

"Hey, Carissa," Isaac said. "I was just calling to let you know what a great time I had on Friday, both with your parents and with you at dinner and the movie. I really enjoyed it. I hope we can do it again."

"Sure, we can. I had a good time, too," Carissa told him. "I just don't know how this surgery is going to go, so I don't know when I'll be up for it again."

"I'll wait." He sounded cheerful and positive. "And, in the meantime, I know where you live. I'll come plop on the couch with you and give you painkillers and soup. That sound good?"

"Sounds perfect." She smiled, wondering how she'd managed to find this one.

"So how are you feeling about pre-op?" he asked. "Nervous?"

"Yeah, a little." That wasn't quite the truth; she was more than a little anxious. "They usually schedule surgery pretty soon after pre-op, so I assume I don't have much time after tomorrow. There'll be blood work, and discussions about past surgeries, then they'll give me a date, probably this week. So, yeah, I'm nervous."

"Yeah, I would be too," he empathized. "Please let me know if I can do anything. I'm still taking care of my mom until the agency can get a decent nurse over here, but I can get away if you need me."

"Thanks, Isaac. I appreciate that. It means a lot." She meant every word of it. It was great to have someone she could count on.

"It's what you do when you care about someone."

"I care about you, too, Isaac," she told him. "I'll call you tomorrow after the appointment and let you know what's going on."

"Sounds good. Goodnight."

They hung up, and Carissa tried to put off falling asleep as long as possible, hoping staring at the clock would give her more time before the appointment. Before she knew it, though, she was awakened by the sun shining through her window. She shoved back her blanket.

Monday was here, and so was pre-op. Maybe she could just lie in bed all day and her parents would forget. A girl could hope.

"Honey, are you up? Mom made pancakes for your big day," Jim called from the hallway.

Or she could just get out of bed and face the day, because obviously no one else was forgetting.

She rolled over as she moaned, "Coming, Dad!" Or some half-words resembling that.

In the kitchen, she found Mom standing over a pan with a pancake in it. Beside her was a giant plate filled with bacon. Well, if she had to do pre-op, this was certainly the way to start. She wheeled herself over and stole a piece of bacon off the plate.

"I'm only letting you get away with that because today is what it is," Sarah said, still facing the stove.

Eyes in the back of her head, as usual, thought Carissa.

"Busted!" Dad laughed from the table.

Carissa munched her bacon, then went back toward the table. Soon, Sarah flopped a big, fluffy pancake onto her plate.

"Syrup is here, butter is there." Sarah pointed out the condiments. "You both already found the bacon. Have at it, guys! I've been sneaking bacon while I cooked, so I'm going to get a shower before we go. Eat up! It's going to be a long day."

Carissa and her dad hardly spoke a word as they shoveled mouthfuls of bacon and pancake into their mouths. Her mom sure knew how to quiet a crowd.

About the time they finished, Sarah came out of the bedroom looking ready for a long day at the hospital, flannel pajama pants and a big t-shirt. She knew from experience that comfort was first and foremost when you were stuck waiting around for doctors.

Carissa took her plate to the sink and went off to get a shower herself. She assumed her dad did the same. She wondered if taking the world's slowest shower might put off the appointment a little longer. Probably not, but a small part of her wasn't above giving it a try. The adult, responsible part of her won out, though, and she finished her shower in a reasonable time, just so she could get all of this over with. She got dressed in her own variation of what her mom was wearing, a Winnie the Pooh two piece pajama set, and went out to meet her doom.

Sarah and Jim were waiting for her when she reached the living room.

"Okay, let's do this!" she said, trying to feel the enthusiasm she'd forced into her voice. She couldn't convince herself, though.

This plain sucked. There was no faking it.

"All right, everybody in the car," Jim said.

The drive to the hospital was quiet. No one seemed to want to talk. Carissa didn't mind. She was in her own head. Her thoughts kept switching from surgery to the possibility of movies on the couch with Isaac. The couch dates almost made the surgery seem worth it. Almost. "God, just take care of me through this. I know You will," she prayed to herself.

CHAPTER 23

Carissa's phone buzzed in her pocket. Who would be calling this early? It was barely 7 a.m.! She glanced at the display on her phone. Isaac.

"Hello, Isaac," she said.

His cheerful voice made her smile. "Hey, I just wanted to let you know I'm thinking about you. I couldn't stop, so I decided to call and make sure you're okay. I hope that's not weird."

"It's not weird," she told him. "We're on our way to the hospital. I'm doing okay, just nervous, but today is blood draws and history. No cutting yet. I'm all right."

"Good," he said. "Well, I have to get my mom ready for her nurse to come. We finally got a new one, so Mom and I will be showing her around, then I'm headed off to class. I'll talk to you after your appointment. Call me."

"Okay," she replied. "Bye, Isaac."

"Bye, Isaac," Dad said loudly from the front seat.

"Bye, Mr. Schultz," Isaac replied, giggling.

"He says bye, Dad."

* * *

The hospital parking lot was crowded, but they managed to find the one handicapped parking spot available. Jim edged the car carefully into the space, then got Carissa's chair and brought it around to her door. She maneuvered into the seat and he pushed her across to the hospital, Sarah following.

Inside, Carissa checked in at the desk and they found a spot for all three of them to sit together in the waiting room.

Carissa kept switching between calm and mini-panic attack. That was all normal. It was what she did before pre-op appointments, ever since she was a little girl.

Jim went to get a drink from the vending machine. Sarah sat beside Carissa's chair, tapping her toes on the floor.

"Show off," Carissa joked. Being paralyzed, she couldn't tap her toes on the floor to get rid of anxiety. Fingers, maybe, but not toes.

Her mother laughed quietly. "Kiddo, only you could still be making jokes at a time like this."

Carissa shrugged. "It's how I deal."

"Well, you deal well." Sarah put her arm around Carissa's shoulder, giving her a hug.

Jim walked back around the corner about the same time the nurse opened the door and called out Carissa's name. They headed toward the exam rooms.

"Here we go!" Carissa thought.

The pre-op interview went as expected. All three of them were ushered into a small room with an exam table against one wall, a desk against the opposite wall, and two chairs against a third wall. A fake plant sat in the corner next to the desk. A very sweet nurse, with her long brown hair rolled up in a bun and wearing pink scrubs, came in with a long line of questioning for Carissa, including her medication list, her medical history, whether she drank or smoked, her sexual history and whether she was active now. Whether there was any chance she could be pregnant. She resisted the urge to throw in a Virgin Mary joke.

All of it was the same as every other time. Carissa was fairly innocent. She didn't need alcohol or drugs. Spina bifida and all the drugs that came with it were enough to keep her uninterested in the drugs and alcohol other kids her age were into. She wasn't into sex. She had promised herself she would wait until marriage. So the interview was pretty boring. The blood tests all came back normal. All that was left was to schedule.

"How's this Friday for you guys?" the nurse asked. "Dr. Brock wanted to get you in as soon as possible to see if he could reverse some of this damage and prevent more. Does that work for you all?"

"Yeah, that'll work," Jim said. He was the only one who might have to get out of work, so it was up to him. Carissa didn't have school anymore, and Sarah stayed home. They scheduled the surgery for that Friday.

"Okay," the nurse told Carissa. "No food after midnight the day before. No breakfast the day of. You can take any meds with a small amount of water the morning of. Just sips, though. Arrive clean. Wash the incision area with anti-bacterial soap and water. Prepare to stay at least three days, probably a week. Bring a list of your medications with you. Arrive at the hospital at 6 a.m. that day. All of this and anything else the doctor wants you to know is here." The nurse handed Carissa a piece of paper with instructions on it.

She'd seen the paper before. This wasn't new, but she read it again, just in case something had changed or she had forgotten something. "Got it!" she said.

"You guys can check out at the front." The nurse got up to usher them out. "We'll see you bright and early on Friday!"

Carissa groaned to herself as she and her parents left the small exam room.

When they got home, Carissa pondered whether or not she was ready to call Isaac with the surgery date. It was so soon. She had half-expected that, and half-hoped they could put it off some. She just wasn't ready for this. And she wasn't sure she was ready to tell Isaac. She would wait until she thought she could do it without getting too emotional. It was too early in their relationship for her to get all teary on him, wasn't it? She wasn't sure. But she wasn't ready to talk.

As if she'd picked up on Carissa's thoughts, Sarah spoke. "Honey, if you want to invite Isaac over for dinner, you can. I'm making turkey burgers," she said, breaking Carissa's train of thought.

Carissa shook her head. "Nah. I'm not sure I'm in the mood for company today. Maybe some other time."

"Okay." Sarah leaned down and kissed Carissa's cheek softly, giving her a hug for courage. "If you change your mind, it's not that big a deal to throw another burger on. Let me know. And I'm here if you want to talk. This will all be okay. It'll be over soon, and you'll be recovering. You and Isaac can have popcorn parties on the couch."

"Okay, Mom. I think I'm just going to go to my room for a bit."

Sarah gave Carissa a gentle smile. "That's fine, honey. Call if you need anything."

Carissa went to her room, and shut the door behind her. Then she cried.

* * *

Once Carissa was in her room, Sarah turned to her husband. "I'm worried about her, Jim."

"I know, but it's just part of her process," Jim comforted her. "You know that. She needs today to accept what's coming. Tomorrow, she'll be back in the fight. She always jumps back in the fight. She just needs her time."

"I know." Sarah sighed. "I just wish there was something we could do besides making her go through all this again."

"We can love her and be there for her. That's what she needs from us." He put his arm around her slumping shoulders. "We can't fix it, but we can be there and be strong for her. She may have to do this, but she doesn't have to do it alone."

"You're right. She's not alone."

CHAPTER 24

Isaac woke up early for class. A new nurse was finally coming, and he'd have to show her the ropes before heading out that morning. Carissa was all he could think about, though. Was she okay? Should he have offered to go with her to the appointment? Were they there in their relationship yet? He didn't want to push, but he wanted to be there for her. This relationship stuff was way harder than College Algebra. But it was also proving much more rewarding.

At almost 11:00, Isaac still hadn't heard from Carissa. Her appointment was at 8 o'clock. Surely she was done by now. He wasn't sure why she hadn't called. He debated whether to call, but decided against it. He would text instead. Maybe that would be easier for her.

"Hey. Just thinking about you. Hope everything went okay. Would like to see you soon." He waited for a response, but none came.

All of this must be so hard for her. Always being the guinea pig… never knowing when her health would fail her… just living life, and then BAM! Spina bifida. He wished he could fix it for her so they could be back in the food court, not studying Algebra over coffee and muffins. He'd do anything to have that back.

For now though, he went to talk to the other woman in his life. He found her in the kitchen, getting a glass of water. Isaac always made sure at least an entire place setting was down out of the cabinets for her, so she didn't always have to ask for help reaching things.

"Hey, Ma," he called out to her as he took a seat at the brown wooden table that had been in their kitchen for as long as he could remember. He had carved his name into it once as a boy, and had gotten his rear end torn up for it when he'd proudly shown it off to his mother. He ran his fingers over the exact spot now and giggled at the memory.

"Hi, baby," she said, taking a long drink of her water and joining him at the table. "Have you heard from Carissa yet?"

"No. I guess she's still at the hospital. Or maybe she just doesn't want to talk. Do you think she's okay?"

"I think she'll talk when she's ready to talk. You just be there when she is." She reached out and pulled his hand into hers.

"I will. I know this must be so hard for her, and I don't know how much to be involved at this point, or whether to back off. I want to be there for her, but I don't want to push, ya know?" He leaned back in his chair, still holding his mom's hand. He ran his fingers over the top of his head, letting out a long breath.

"I know, baby. Just let her lead. Let her know you're there. She'll come to you for comfort if she needs you. You really like this girl, don't you?"

"I do, Ma. I really do." He got up from the table and poured a glass of water for himself. He leaned against the white kitchen counter. "She's something. It's important to me that I do right by her."

"Baby, like I told you before, you just be the man I know you can be. You'll be all right."

CHAPTER 25

C arissa sat on her bed, thinking of ways to tell Isaac she'd be out of the dating scene for a while. Could she ask him to wait for her? Was that fair? Or should she just tell him to move on and find a girl without so much baggage?

She didn't want to put him through this. This was her problem. He hadn't signed up for a "sick" girlfriend who might need regular procedures for the rest of her life. He had signed up for a pre-law student with a future ahead of her, who liked to eat chocolate chip muffins while pretending to study Algebra. Surgery was surely not part of his romantic plans for them.

Her phone buzzed and knocked her out of her thoughts. It was him. He was thinking about her, probably wondering why she didn't call. He wanted to see her soon.

Why did he insist on being so amazingly present? Should she call him? She probably should. This was so hard, though. He did not deserve this. He deserved a girl who could go out and do things with him. This was the beginning of their relationship. Things should be easier. He shouldn't have to put up with this so soon.

She decided to call. He deserved to know what was going on. He could decide for himself whether he would hang in there with her. Part of her hoped he would. Part of her hoped, for his sake, that he would just hit the road. She pressed the button to call him.

It didn't take long for him to answer, and she rushed into what she wanted to say. "Hey, it's Carissa. I'm sorry I didn't call sooner. Rough day," she blurted out. "Look, I got scheduled for surgery. It's soon. Friday. I'll understand if you just want to take a break until I'm past all this, or even just break it off altogether. You didn't sign up for this."

"What? What are you talking about? Break it off?" Isaac asked. "Carissa, I knew when I met you that we may run into some things. I'm not running from this. I told you I'd be there with muffins on your couch. I wasn't just talking to hear myself talk. I want to be with you. ALL of you! The muffin parts, the part that hates math, the surgery part. All of you. I don't burn off at the first sign of a challenge.

"My dad did that to my mom," he went on, "and I won't be that man. I understood when I approached you that first day that we might have issues that other couples don't. I did sign up for this, and I don't plan on signing off, unless you run me off and, last I checked, you kind of suck at running. You're not getting away!"

"Um... well... Okay then. Mom wanted to know if you wanted to come for dinner tonight. Do you like turkey burgers?" she asked.

"So far, I like anything that comes out of your mama's kitchen. I'll be there."

"Great," she said. "I'll let her know. We can discuss the surgery over dinner."

"Sounds like a plan," he said, excitement in his voice. "I'm looking forward to it."

After they hung up, Carissa went out to tell Sarah, trying to decide how she was feeling. Isaac sure was starting to sound like he really wanted to stick around. Could he really be this good? She wasn't sure, but she was running out of reasons to doubt him.

"Hey, Mom," she said, wheeling into the kitchen where her mom was prepping for dinner. "I talked to Isaac, and he wants a burger. He'll be here for dinner."

"Great," Sarah answered, turning to face Carissa. "Four burgers, coming up! Do you guys want fries or onion rings?"

"Oh! Onion rings sound great!" Carissa said.

"You got it," Sarah told her, bending down to get an onion out of the refrigerator. "Are you feeling better about everything?"

"Yeah, kinda. It's still scary, though. I guess we just get through it like everything else." Carissa grabbed a butcher knife out of the drawer to help cut the onion.

"Yep. That's my girl!" Sarah beamed at her daughter, pride sticking out all over her. "You get through everything just fine, once you get past yourself. Your dad and I know you'll do great."

"Only because I have you guys." Carissa grinned back at Sarah.

"Sweetie, you'll always have us behind you, no matter what comes." She handed the onion over to Carissa.

"I know, Mom." Carissa finished chopping the onion and said, "I'm going to go get ready for Isaac to come. Clean my room and shower. I'll be back."

"Okay, honey. See you around dinner time."

CHAPTER 26

"Jim, Isaac is coming over for dinner tonight," Sarah said, walking into the living room where Jim sat watching television. "I invited him. Try to wear something besides your bath robe."

"Ha! He only gets to be a guest once," Jim laughed, eyes still fixed on the baseball game he was watching. "This time he gets the full Schultz welcome. You should wear curlers in your hair."

"Jim!" Sarah was annoyed and amused at the same time.

"What? Tell me you don't want to embarrass the girl a little... lighten things up around here. It's been a rough week." Jim stood up and put his hands on his hips, an impish grin on his face.

"All the more reason to act like humans when her boyfriend comes over," Sarah told him, coming over to put her arms around his waist.

"Did she call him that? Boyfriend? Is he her boyfriend?" Jim asked, embracing her.

"I don't know, Jim," she replied. "I don't even know if they know, but I know he kissed her on the porch the other night when he brought her home from the movie."

"Kissed her? Wow. In my book, that makes him the boyfriend. At least he better be!" Sarah felt his chest tighten under her grip.

"Well, it's really not our business. He's a nice kid. Let them work it out." She held him tighter, trying to tame the beast.

"Uh-huh." Jim replied.

"Jim."

"Yeah, I got you. Let them work it out. I won't say anything."

It wasn't long before Isaac was knocking on the door. Jim let go of Sarah and went to answer it. "Hey, Isaac, come on in," Jim said. "I'll go get Carissa."

"Thank you, sir." Isaac stepped through the door. "Nice to see you again."

* * *

Jim went to get Carissa for dinner, and Isaac went into the kitchen to greet Sarah and see if she needed any help finishing dinner. "Can I do anything, Mrs. S?" he asked.

"Sure, Isaac, so nice of you to ask." She handed him a tomato and a knife. "You can slice this while I finish up these onion rings."

"Sounds like a plan!" Isaac got to cutting. "So how's Carissa doing with all of this? Is she okay? It took her a long time to call me today after her appointment."

"She's all right, Isaac," Sarah said, adding seasoning to the onions in her bowl. "She just has her process. She gets depressed when something comes up then, before long, she's back on the horse. It has nothing to do with you. Please know that. She really likes you. She's just not used to having a boy around who cares so much."

"Oh, I care," he said. "I care a lot. She's really special. I just want her to be okay."

"She will be. Her father and I will be there for her through the whole thing, and I know it would mean a lot if you showed up some, too, just to take her mind off things." She patted him on the back.

"I'll be around as much as you and Mr. S will allow, ma'am." He smiled at her.

"That's good. She'll need a friend. Recovery from surgery is long and boring. I'll buy plenty of popcorn for you guys to eat while you watch movies on the couch. It's not a date, and you won't get to kiss her if her dad has anything to say about it, but it's something." She gave him a knowing eye.

Isaac could feel his cheeks get hot. Had she seen them the other night on the porch? "Well, something with Carissa, even if it's not a date, is better than anything without Carissa. I'll take it."

"Good man," Sarah said.

Just then, Carissa and Jim came into the kitchen.

"Hey, Isaac!"

Isaac greeted Carissa with a hug—a "friend" hug. "Hey, are you doing okay? Your mom says we can have popcorn fights on the couch after your surgery."

"Well, hearing that, I'm about seventy-five percent better!" Carissa grinned.

"Good!" Isaac looked pleased at himself. "That's what I'm here for."

"Well, that and delicious turkey burgers, right?" Sarah piped in.

"Yes, ma'am. Those, too!"

"Everybody sit down," she said. "I'll bring them out."

Sarah went back into the kitchen, and the sounds of a drawer opening and silverware clinking were followed by her returning with a platter full of burgers on buns and a bowl of onion rings that smelled delicious. She put the food in the center of the table.

Everyone sat, and Jim said the blessing. When he was done, Isaac asked, "So, surgery on Friday. I was wondering, if you guys don't mind, could I come? I don't want to impose, or place myself where I don't belong, but I'd really like to be there for Carissa if that's okay with you, Mr. and Mrs. Schultz."

"You don't have to do that," Carissa responded.

"I want to," he insisted. "This is not a thing I feel like I have to do. I want to be there for you."

"Okay, but it's boring." She shrugged, looking at him with surprise.

"I like boring," Isaac told her. "Mr. Schultz, is it okay if I come and hang around?"

"Sure, Isaac. That's fine. We'll pick you up that morning. It'll be early, probably around 5:30 a.m." Jim replied.

"Works for me. As long as I'm not sitting around waiting for a phone call all day. I don't think I could handle not knowing what was up."

They passed around the food and began to eat, talking about Carissa's upcoming surgery and Isaac's classes. Dinner was finished quickly.

"It must have been good, huh?" Sarah started to collect dishes from the table. "I didn't hear a peep out of anyone the whole meal!"

"Yes, ma'am, it was outstanding," Isaac replied, wiping his face with a napkin.

"It was great, hon," Jim paid a compliment to his wife.

"So good, Mom," chimed Carissa.

"Well, everybody help me clean up, and maybe we'll play a board game in the living room. Hey, we have four. Maybe teams!"

Everyone agreed, and got to cleaning up. Sarah rinsed the dishes, then handed them to Carissa, who placed them in the dishwasher. Jim and Isaac cleared the rest of the table of condiments and minimal leftovers.

Team charades, guys against girls, was a hit. At one point, Isaac impersonated a chicken with its head cut off by running around in circles, hacking at his own neck. He had everyone laughing hysterically, but Jim didn't get it and they lost that round. Carissa managed to win a round for the girls by pretending her wheelchair was a horse for "Horse and Rider." Sarah and Carissa won by two points in the end.

"Team Lady Schultz for life. Yeah, baby!" Sarah yelled, jumping up and down in victory.

"She's not competitive at all," Carissa said, throwing a pillow that Sarah deftly caught.

"I can tell," replied Isaac, grinning.

"Yeah, these girls are the reigning champs of just about every guys-on-girls game ever played here in the Schultz house. Of course, it doesn't help that I'm usually the only guy," Jim admitted.

"Well, it looks like all I did was contribute to their winning streak," replied Isaac.

Carissa's dad laughed out loud. "They're tough competition. The guys will prevail someday."

"Yes, sir!" And Isaac hoped Carissa would keep him around for that day. He was starting to like her family as much as he liked her. He looked at the clock and rose from his seat. "Well, I have to get home and take care of my mom. She'll be waiting up for me, and I need to see how her new nurse is working out. Carissa, do you want to walk me out?"

Carissa looked up at him with a smile. "Sure!"

Once they were alone, Isaac leaned down and kissed her, without asking this time. He lingered on her lips for a moment without moving. Then he straightened and said, "Goodnight, Carissa. I didn't want to do that in front of your dad, and this may be the last chance I get to do it for a while without him watching. I won't do it with him watching. I'm not trying to get punched."

"Goodnight, Isaac," she giggled, wrapping her arms around his neck for a quick hug. "I'll see you Friday, if not before."

* * *

Carissa sat on the front porch for a bit, just taking everything in. Here she was, about to have this huge surgery and, for the first time since Kayla died, she would have someone besides her parents in her corner. It felt good. Isaac felt good in general.

Kissing Isaac wasn't so bad, either.

She went back inside to find her parents snuggling on the couch watching a movie. She turned down the hall and went to do her nighttime routine. "I'm headed to bed, lovebirds. Goodnight."

"Lovebirds? Look who's talking!" Sarah replied.

"Goodnight, Carissa," Jim said. "Tell that boy I know what he's up to on that porch. I was a boy once, too."

Carissa felt her cheeks heat up as she headed to her room.

Sarah's voice followed her. "Go to bed, Carissa. I'll handle Dad."

She left before Sarah could change her mind.

CHAPTER 27

Isaac drove home that night, excited about what the future might hold. He was really starting to feel at home with the Schultzs. Mr. Schultz was kind of hard on him, but he understood. Carissa was a special girl, and he didn't want her hurt.

Isaac didn't want her hurt, either. He hoped he never did anything to hurt her. Whatever happened, he wanted her happy. He thought about her surgery on Friday, and wondered what it would be like to see her in a hospital bed. That would be rough. She was always so active, and mostly perky. Seeing her lying in pain was definitely going to be different, and probably painful, but he'd do it. He was pretty sure he would do anything for her. He'd never felt this way about a girl before. He was hooked and he knew it would be hard, but he honestly couldn't wait to be stuck on the couch with her for a few weeks, bringing her soup. Anything she was involved in sounded like a good time.

Isaac arrived home just in time to see the new nurse pull out of the driveway. She waved as she saw him pull in. Isaac waved back, parked, and made his way up the driveway to the ramp that was his mother's way into the house. He opened the glass-paned door and walked into the house, through the dark living room with the ugly red sofa they'd owned for too many years. The television was off, as were all the lights in the house.

Inside her bedroom, he found his mom, nicely tucked into bed.

"Hey, Ma, how's the new nurse?" Isaac gave his mom a kiss. "She seems nice. Waved goodbye as I pulled up. Is she good? Did she do everything like you asked? Do you need anything?"

"She's great, Isaac!" His mom smiled, her face happy and contented. "Much better than Cindy, and I don't even think I scared her."

"That's good. You gotta stop scaring off the nurses." Isaac laughed at her. "The agency is running out of them."

"How's Carissa?" his mom asked.

"She's okay." He shrugged. "Nervous about everything and I don't blame her. I'm nervous, too, and I'm not even the one getting cut. But she seems to be handling it well. She's strong."

"That's good." She glanced up at him. "Tell her I'm praying for her and, since I'm spending so much of my prayer time on her, bring her over sometime. I'm praying for this girl you haven't proven exists yet." She shook her finger at him. "What's that about, boy? Bring her to me. Let me get eyeballs on this girl you seem so gaga over. The house is even accessible. She'd be perfectly comfortable here."

"All right, Ma, I'll bring her over."

"Before Friday," she said. "I don't want to wait to meet her. She seems like a good one. I want eyeballs on her soon."

"Okay, Ma." He leaned over and gave her a goodnight hug and kiss.

"Go to sleep, boy. I'll see you in the morning."

"Goodnight, Ma. I love you!"

"I love you, too, Isaac."

Isaac went to his room and got ready for bed, thinking about Carissa the whole time. Yeah, he was gone.

He was pretty sure he loved her.

CHAPTER 28

J im and Sarah stood in the living room talking about the evening. "I can't even lie. I like that kid," Jim admitted when Carissa was out of earshot. "He needs to quit kissing my daughter on the porch, but I like him."

"Jim," Sarah admonished, "Carissa likes the kissing. If the kissing stops, we lose the boy. If you like the boy, the kissing stays. Sorry to have to be the one to disappoint you." She placed a loving hand on his chest.

"Oh, stop. That's my daughter!" He pulled back playfully.

"I'm just saying." She wrapped her arm around him. "And, in case you don't remember, she's my daughter, too."

"I know," he said, pulling her in closer.

"Okay. They aren't kissing." Sarah grinned at him a little impishly. "They're planning to overthrow the government. Is that better?"

"Much," he conceded, "but what if she falls in love and he

realizes the spina bifida and all that comes with it is just too much? It's too much for us sometimes. I just don't want to see her get her heart broken. I'd much rather they overthrow the government than have to watch my little girl get hurt."

"Believe what you have to." She patted him on the back. "I'm afraid too, but we can't protect her from everything. Isaac seems like a nice guy, but if you have to tell yourself they're not kissing out there, go ahead and lie to yourself." She smiled up at him.

"It's what I do best." Jim replied. "But, no, really, I like him. I almost hope he sticks around for a while. Carissa seems happy, in spite of everything she's facing."

"What if he sticks around forever?" Sarah raised her eyebrows, the question hanging between them.

"Stop it!" he said one more time.

"I'm just saying." She shrugged. "A mom knows things."

"Well, stop knowing," Jim told her. "My little girl is too young for forever."

"Okay, Jim. She's overthrowing the government. That's all. She's not in love with him."

"That's so much better."

"Whatever you say, dear." She slipped her arm through his and pulled him toward the sofa. " Let's watch this crazy movie you picked."

They cozied into each other, both of them falling asleep on the couch.

CHAPTER 29

The week was going fast. It was already Wednesday, and Carissa was feeling Friday coming in much too quickly, but Isaac had called earlier and invited her to come over for dinner.

"Mom, do you need the car for anything tonight?"

Her mom looked up from the paper she was reading. "No, baby, why?"

"Isaac invited me over to his house for dinner tonight," Carissa said. "His mom wants to meet me. Can I go?"

"Sure," Sarah said with a smile. "Just don't stay out too late, and be a lady."

"Will do, Mom!"

Carissa went to get ready. She was nervous about meeting Ms. Carter, and she wanted to make a good impression. At least they both used wheelchairs. It was hard to convince parents you were a good choice for a girlfriend from a chair. She'd tried it before. At least she had that going for her this time. Ms. Carter would see another person, not just a chair. Still, Carissa's nerves were jumping. Ms. Carter had raised a man all on her own. Chair or not, she was strong, and might still be a tough critic.

Carissa showered and put on what she thought was a proper, "meet the parents" outfit, said a little prayer that she wouldn't totally screw this up, and headed out the door to Isaac's house. Because she had never been there, her navigation system was her best friend.

Isaac lived on the other side of town in a small red brick house that was in need of repair. At least she knew his house would be accessible for her wheelchair. That wasn't always the case when visiting friends, or even family.

She pulled up in the concrete driveway, set her chair outside the car door, dropped into it, and headed to the door. On each side of the walkway, there were beautiful pink and purple flowers. Carissa wondered if Isaac or his mom had planted them. She knew it would be a lot of work to plant flowers from a wheelchair, but she didn't see Isaac as the horticultural type.

She knocked and waited. It seemed like she sat there forever with her heart pounding in her chest. Then Isaac appeared.

"Hey, come in. Ma, Carissa is here!" he called.

Carissa entered the house and Ms. Carter came from the kitchen wearing a long black dress with a large red flower pattern down the front. She was short and stocky, like Isaac, and very dark. "Hello, Carissa. I've heard so much about you." A wide, genuine smile lit up her face. "Don't worry, Isaac can't think of a bad thing to tell me. Come on in. Dinner is just about ready. Isaac, show the lady to the table."

Isaac led Carissa to a square, wooden, black painted table with bowls and spoons already set out. There was a flower vase in the center with a single yellow rose. He moved a black wooden chair out of the way so she could scoot in.

Carissa moved over and reached out to shake Isaac's mother's hand. "Thank you for having me, Ms. Carter. I really appreciate the invite."

The other woman's hand was warm and strong. "Honey, call me Betty. I don't do all that formal stuff. We're real low key around here."

"Okay, Betty, I will. Thanks!" Carissa followed Betty, with Isaac behind, into the dining room. The two women rolled their chairs up to the table, and Isaac helped the nurse bring dinner over.

"Well, Ms. Carter, now that you have Isaac here, and your company, I think I'll head on out. I'll see you bright and early tomorrow!" the nurse announced.

"Okay, honey," Betty said. "See you tomorrow. Thank you for your help!"

With dinner sitting in the center of the table, Isaac said the blessing, and they all started eating their meal of shepherd's pie.

"It's delicious, Ma," Isaac said.

"Yes, ma'am, really good. Thank you!" Carissa agreed.

"I'm glad you both like it," Betty said, delighted the meal was okay. "So, Carissa, tell me about you. Isaac says your major is pre-law. That's some pretty heavy stuff."

"Yes, ma'am," Carissa told her. "I'm not sure of all the specifics yet, but I want to do something in the disability law realm." Carissa leaned forward, eager to share her dreams with this woman she had so much in common with. "Something that makes a huge difference, you know, kind of like the ADA did for us. I just feel like I was born into this chair life to make something happen. I don't believe in coincidence. I'm in this chair for a reason. I want to do what I can with it."

Betty sat back in her chair. "Wow! You have some pretty big

goals there," she exclaimed. "You know, I was in some of those protests for the ADA when I was about your age… or older… We won't talk about how old I was, but I was part of it. Aside from Isaac being born, it was one of the best experiences of my life. We were all on fire. I could introduce you to some of the people I still hang around with. You might catch some inspiration. Some of them are still in the government scene, still moving and shaking things in Washington for us. Would you be interested in meeting some of them?"

"Oh, yes, ma'am." Carissa was thrilled at the thought of getting involved with this group of people. "It might have to be after my surgery, though. That's coming up pretty quick, and they're saying I might have a long recovery, but I'd definitely love to meet some of the minds behind the ADA. How exciting!"

"Who knows? You might be out there rallying for your own laws someday. That would be exciting!" Betty beamed. "I'd be right there beside you. I'd love to jump back into that fire again."

Carissa saw the nostalgia in Betty's eyes. It lit something inside her.

The rest of dinner was filled with Betty telling Carissa all about her time as an activist for the ADA. She talked about being right there at the Capitol building the day the Americans With Disabilities Act was passed, and how excited she was. She talked about seeing the changes come all around town: wheelchair ramps, elevators, handrails. Disabled people were finally seeing the changes they needed to navigate the world. It still wasn't perfect, but Betty told Carissa it was so much better than it used to be. Isaac could hardly get a word in between his mom and his girlfriend, and he didn't look like he minded.

When dinner was over, they all helped clear the table, and Isaac offered to do the dishes.

"I'll help!" Carissa chimed in.

"Well, then, this old lady is going to plop herself in front of the television. You guys come on in when you're done." Betty went to the living room.

"I like your mom," Carissa told Isaac when they were alone.

Isaac rinsed a plate in the sink before putting it into the dishwasher. "She likes you, too. I can tell."

"Good. You want a lady like her to like you," Carissa said, handing him the next plate. "She's really something."

"You know, Carissa, you're really something, too," Isaac said, smiling down at her. "I really like you a lot. In fact, I think I might be growing to more than like you."

Carissa thought she was going to scrub the pattern off the plate in her hands.

Isaac continued, "I think I love you. I've never felt like this around anyone else in my life. I can't wait to talk to you. It doesn't matter what happens in my day. As long as you're involved, I'm good. You brighten up everything. You're the first thing I think about every morning, and the last thing I think about at night. I really think... no, I know... Carissa, I love you." Carissa felt the plate slip in her hand. She felt lucky she didn't drop it, the way her heart was pounding. She managed to put it down in the sink before it fell to the floor.

"I love you, too, Isaac. I've never felt this way either," Carissa admitted. "I don't know how to act around you, and yet I do, because even when I'm all nervous and weird, you make it so easy."

To ease the tension, Isaac picked up the faucet sprayer, and sprinkled Carissa right in the face.

"Isaac!" she screamed.

Betty's voice came from the other room. "Isaac! What are you doing in there? Treat a lady like a lady!"

"Sorry, Ma!" he yelled back to his mom, but he didn't look sorry.

Carissa and Isaac both laughed. This was love.

After the dishes were finished, Carissa and Isaac joined his mother in the living room.

"Thank you so much for dinner, Ms... Um... Betty," Carissa said. "It was delicious."

"You're welcome, Carissa. You're welcome to come back for more any time. We have dinner just about every night around here, and I can never manage to cook for just the two of us. My mama always cooked for the whole neighborhood, and so do I. We'll always have plenty."

Carissa smiled at that thought. "Thank you, ma'am. I'm sure I'll be around for more. Isaac, I should probably get going. I told my parents I wouldn't be out too late."

"I'll walk you out," he replied.

"It was nice having you, Carissa," said Betty. "Like I said, we always have more than enough. You're welcome to come back any time. We'll see you later."

"Yes, ma'am. I'll be back." Carissa meant it, too.

On the porch, Isaac sat down on an Adirondack chair so he could be face to face with Carissa. "I meant what I said in there. I love you, and I want you to know that I take us seriously. I know you think I can't handle this spina bifida thing, and the surgery coming up, but I'm in this. I'm not like other eighteen-year-old guys. I'm with you. I'm not going anywhere."

"I love you, too, Isaac, and I trust you. I'll see you Friday morning." She leaned in to kiss him before leaving.

CHAPTER 30

Friday was here before anyone could blink. Carissa woke up to the sound of her alarm clock blaring earlier than usual. She slammed her hand down on it, and immediately remembered everything that was to happen today. "Oh, man. I can't do this. I'm so not ready." But she hopped out of the bed and jumped in the shower to wash with her anti-bacterial soap, as instructed. Upon finishing, she went out to the living room to find her parents, but they weren't there. She hoped they would be out of their bedroom soon. They didn't have a lot of spare time if they were going to pick up Isaac.

"Hey, kiddo! You ready for this?" Sarah said as she came into the living room.

"Nope!" Carissa said.

"Good! Me, neither. Let's do it!" Sarah headed for the kitchen.

"Sounds like a plan. Is Dad almost ready?" Carissa asked anxiously. "We have to go get Isaac."

"Dad's getting dressed now. Don't worry," Sarah announced from the kitchen. "We have time. I gotta start coffee, though, or I'm not gonna make it through the day!"

Carissa heard the usual morning preparations going on as Sarah started the coffee, just as Jim came out of the bedroom.

"Hey, Dad! Mom's on the coffee already."

"That's good," Jim said. "I'll need some for the road. Why don't you call Isaac and tell him we're heading out in about ten minutes. Make sure he's up."

"Okay." Carissa punched in Isaac's number as Jim followed the smell of fresh coffee into the kitchen.

When Isaac answered, Carissa said, "Hey, Isaac, we're leaving in about ten to pick you up. You ready?"

"Yeah," he told her. "I'm waiting on the couch. Text me when you're close so no one has to come up and get me. See you soon. I love you."

"I love you, too." She ended the call.

Sarah came flying out of the kitchen and into the bedroom, where she dressed lightning fast. She was ready to head out before Carissa could blink.

"Okay, everybody, pile up! Let's get this party started!" Jim said, and they headed out to the car.

In the car, Jim said, "Let's say a quick prayer." They bowed their heads to pray for Carissa's surgery and recovery.

The ride was silent on the way to get Isaac. Carissa didn't know if it was sleep deprivation, nerves, or a combination of the two, but no one said anything until Isaac got in the car.

"Hey, Isaac," Sarah said, her voice sounding sleepy.

"Hi, Mrs. Schultz, good morning! You, too, Mr. Schultz."

Isaac looked over at Carissa. She looked beautiful this early. Sleepy eyes, hair kind of a mess. It was a natural beauty she had without trying. "Hey, you. Doing okay?"

"Yeah," she said, "just ready to get it over with, and a little hungry. No food since dinner last night."

"Well, I'll get you a decent meal as soon as they'll let me." He grinned at her, disgustingly chipper.

"Sounds good," she agreed glumly. "A cheeseburger?"

"I'll get right on that," he said. "It'll have to be hospital, though. No car."

"Ugh. I'll take it," she told him. "I'll probably be starving when I wake up, so it won't matter."

The car went silent again. There didn't seem to be a lot to say. When they arrived at the hospital, everybody got out, almost reluctantly.

"Come on, sleepy head. Let's go," Sarah said.

"I'm coming, I'm coming." Carissa moaned.

Carissa got checked in at the surgical desk, and they waited until a short, red-headed woman wearing green scrubs came out to get her.

"Carissa?" she said. "I'm Sandy. Come on back. I'll get you all dressed up in your party dress, and then I'll bring your family back when you're all set. Looks like everything's running right on time, so you shouldn't have to wait long."

Carissa followed Sandy back to a hospital room where a gown, booties, and a paper hat waited for her. "Do you need any help transferring or getting any of this stuff on?"

"No, ma'am." Carissa gave her a wry look. "I've got it. I'm a pro. Thanks, though."

"Well, all right then." Sandy smiled. "I'll leave you to it. Here's your call button if you need anything. Oh, and pee in this cup when you get a chance."

Carissa stopped her before she left. "Do you have a catheter?"

she asked. "I need one to pee. Non-latex."

Most people with spina bifida were highly susceptible to developing a latex allergy. Carissa wasn't allergic yet but, because she was exposed so much, she used precautions where she could.

"Oh, yes, ma'am." Sandy apologized. "I'm sorry. I should have known that with the spina bifida and all. I'll bring the catheter."

Carissa smiled. "It's fine. Not everyone thinks of it."

"I'll be right back."

Carissa was left alone with her thoughts and her hospital booties. She put everything on, including the little gown that didn't cover anything, and climbed onto the bed. She didn't understand the point of those. She might as well be naked when Isaac came back there.

Sandy popped back in with the catheter just as Carissa was getting settled on the hospital bed.

"Do you need any help with this? I assume not. You're probably better at it than me."

Carissa took it. "No, ma'am. No help needed. I'm pretty good at it. Thanks!"

"Okay, then. You okay if I go get your family? You should be settled back in bed before we get back."

"That's fine." Sandy left, and Carissa went to empty her bladder into the cup. The nurse had been right about the timing. Just about the time she got settled in the bed again, Isaac and her parents walked in the room.

"I like your hat," Isaac smirked.

She blew him a raspberry. "Ha, very funny."

The nurse came back with all the equipment needed to start Carissa's IV.

"Great," Carissa thought.

"Which arm do we like?" the nurse asked.

"I have a good vein on the left arm… riiiiight here." Carissa grinned. She didn't know where Sandy got the "we" from. No one was shoving a needle in her arm.

"Works for me!" Sandy laughed. "I'll take the one the pro knows!"

She rubbed Carissa's arm with alcohol, let it dry, then stuck the needle in. Carissa winced; she hated IVs. Needles were never fun, no matter how "pro" you were.

"Okay, all done. I'm going to start some fluids," Sandy announced. "Are you nervous? I can ask the doctor to give you something to calm you."

"Yes, ma'am." She needed calming.

"I'll go get that."

"Thank you." Carissa laid back in the bed.

The nurse left them alone in the room. There was some light chatter between Jim and Isaac, but Sarah and Carissa didn't talk much. They just waited. Soon, medical professionals were coming in and out non-stop to get information out of Carissa before surgery, so there wasn't much time to say anything else.

The different medical staff people asked Carissa the same line of questions about six times. She wondered why the first guy didn't just come in, ask all the questions, and then deliver the message to everyone else. She knew, though, that they were looking for discrepancies. They wanted to make sure she gave the same answers every time so they could know they weren't getting false information, whether by mistake or on purpose. One false answer could be life or death when you were unconscious on an operating table.

Carissa had no reason to lie, so she gave the same answers repeatedly until she thought she might forget the answers altogether. During all the questioning, the nurse came in and gave Carissa the calming medicine she had asked for, and her nerves finally settled.

"Thank God for modern medicine, huh? I wish they had some of that for me," Sarah said.

"I wish they had this stuff for everyone," Carissa replied.

Just then, a short, bald man in blue scrubs came in, introduced himself as the limo driver, and told everyone it was time to get the show going.

"Okay, kiddo!" Jim said. "Show 'em what ya got!"

"I love you, Carissa. You'll do great." Sarah kissed her on the forehead and hugged her as best she could with all the paraphernalia in and around her daughter.

Isaac walked over, tears in his eyes, and leaned in and kissed her. "I love you," he whispered.

"I love you, too," she whispered back. "Ha! You kissed me in front of my dad!" And the "limo driver" rolled Carissa away.

"Now we wait," Jim said.

"Yep," Sarah responded.

"Well, does anybody want some breakfast?" Jim asked. "Carissa won't mind now. We won't be eating in front of her. Let's go down and see what kind of hospital slop we can pull together."

Sarah and Isaac agreed, and they headed toward the hospital cafeteria.

They managed to find some over-done scrambled eggs, some under-done bacon, and some semi-warm coffee. It was about as good as it got for hospital food. Ketchup would make up the difference between the slop it was and the food they wanted it to be. Enough cream and sugar would make the coffee palatable. At least they could hope.

Isaac tried to pay for his, but Jim covered it when they got to the register.

"Thank you, sir. You didn't have to."

"It's no problem, son. I've got it."

They took a table near the window and started in on the breakfast pretending to be breakfast.

"Mmmm… hospital food," Sarah joked. "We've had too much of this stuff in our lifetimes, huh, Jim?"

"Yes, we have," he replied. "I think I'm almost starting to tolerate it. Is that a bad sign? Do you think I'm catching something?"

"Probably. Stick out your tongue." She held up her spoon like a thermometer.

Jim shook his head. "Not gonna happen."

"Well, I can't check if you won't let me see it. Guess you'll just have to be a sicko."

"Fine with me!" Jim laughed.

They finished breakfast and still had some time to kill, so they went down to the hospital garden to sit and take in a view and smell non-antiseptic air.

Jim looked over at Isaac. "Isaac, I want you to know I think it means a lot to Carissa that you came today. And it means a lot to us, too. You're quite the gentleman," Jim said.

Isaac glanced away for just a second, then locked eyes with Carissa's father. "I wouldn't miss this, sir. I like Carissa a lot, and I wouldn't want her to go through this alone. I don't want to be anywhere else today," he said. "I don't know what I else I'd be doing if I wasn't here. I'd probably be pacing my room until someone called me. I'd rather know right away that she's okay and comfortable."

"Well, we appreciate it," Jim said, laying a hand on Isaac's shoulder. "She really likes having your support."

They sat in the garden and looked at the flowers some more, Sarah identifying each one for the guys. As the morning went on, it got too hot to be outside, so they went back to the waiting room.

Shortly after they arrived, the nurse came out to update them on Carissa's progress.

"Carissa is doing fine. We're just closing up now, and she'll go to recovery for a little while. At that point, Dr. Brock will come out and tell you things from his perspective," the surgery room nurse told them. "When she starts to wake up a little bit, we'll come get you so you can go in and see her, two at a time. Everything has gone well to this point, though, and we don't expect any complications. She should be done really soon."

"Thank you," Sarah said.

The nurse walked away, and they simultaneously breathed a sigh of relief. It was good to know it was almost over and she had done well. No one expected less out of Carissa, but it was still good to hear it was true.

"Man, I'm glad we're on the downhill side of this," Jim admitted.

"Yeah," Isaac agreed.

"I just want to see my girl," Sarah replied.

It took about another hour for the doctor to come out. When he did, he took a seat in the middle of them to tell them how the surgery had gone.

"Carissa looks good. She went through the surgery well, and I think she might regain all of her previous movement and sensation. Her bladder may come back to normal as well. Of course, everything is kind of 'wait and see' at this point, but I'm optimistic." Dr. Brock paused. "I'm glad Dr. Taylor caught what he did on his end; otherwise, this could have gone on for much longer and been much more damaging. Honestly, I think it went as well as we could expect. She could be out of here in as little as a few days, depending on how well her spine recovers. I expect some outpatient rehabilitation for a while, but things look really good.

You should be able to see her in a half-hour or so. Any questions for me?"

"No. Thank you so much, Doctor," Sarah said. "I just want to see my baby again."

"You will soon," Dr. Brock assured her. "Let me go back and check on how things are progressing, and I'll send a nurse out as soon as you can come back."

Dr. Brock left and, once again, a sigh of relief filled the room. It had gone well. She would only stay a couple of days. They really couldn't ask for more. All this was definitely good news.

It wasn't long before a nurse came out and told them they could come back to see Carissa, but only two at a time, so as not to overwhelm her or crowd the room.

"You guys go back. I'll wait," Isaac volunteered. "You're her parents. I'm sure she wants to see you."

"Are you sure?" Jim said. "I don't mind waiting. I mean, not forever. That's my little girl back there, but I can wait for a bit."

"No, no," Isaac protested. "That's okay. Go on back. She'll want her dad."

Sarah hugged Isaac, and she and Jim headed back to see Carissa. When they got to her room, she was drowsy, but awake.

"Hi, honey. Are you in any pain?" Jim asked.

"A little. Not too much." Her words were slurred and a little slow. "Just tired. How did I do?"

"Dr. Brock said you did great, and he expects you to return to normal. He said you'll probably be out of here in a few days," Sarah told her.

"Good. I want to go home."

"Hold on there, kiddo! We don't even know if you can still walk!" Jim said.

"Dad!" Carissa half-yelled, half-mumbled through the

anesthesia working its way out of her system.

"Jim, that's not funny," Sarah scolded.

"It's kinda funny," Carissa giggled. "Hey, did Isaac stay?"

"Yes, he did," Jim said, his voice positive and almost admiring. "But they would only let us back two at a time. He's in the waiting room. I'll go get him before your mom slaps me for making more jokes."

Jim left the room and went to get Isaac. "Someone is asking for you," he told Isaac.

"Is she? How does she look?" Isaac looked concerned.

Jim smiled. "Good. Tired, but good. Not too much pain."

"That's fantastic." Isaac got up. "I'm gonna go back."

"Okay, I'll be here," Jim said.

Isaac walked down the hall to the post-op rooms and found Carissa's name on one of the doors. Hesitantly, he opened it. It would be hard to see her like this, but it would be harder not to see her. He peeked around the corner. "Hey, can I come in?"

"Come on!" Sarah said, from closer to the bed.

He walked in and stopped. Carissa looked so tiny and frail in the bed. She had always been tiny, but the bed and blankets, along with all the equipment around her, made her look even smaller.

"Hey, you," Carissa said, smiling up at him. "I'm okay. It hurts a little, but I'm fine. Don't worry about me. You look worried."

"I just really care, and it's harder to see you like this than I thought." He moved to the bedside and reached for Carissa's hand.

"I'm gonna step outside and let you guys talk," Sarah announced. "Isaac, if you need anything, or if she needs anything, I'll be in the waiting room."

"Yes, ma'am," he replied.

"Isaac, you can go if you want to," Carissa said. "My dad can take you home."

"I wouldn't even consider that," he said, his voice solemn. "I'm here as long as you and your parents will allow. I might have to go home at some point and get clothes, but I'm not leaving for long. I just wouldn't." He squeezed her hand. "I don't know how I'd sit at home and not be able to see you."

"Okay," she grinned, obviously pleased at his response. "You can stay then, but I won't be very entertaining."

"I'm not looking for entertainment," he said. "I'm here to support you."

"Well, then your first order of duty is to find me a soda."

"Can you have that yet?" he wondered, his voice tentative.

"I don't know. Why?" She was indignant. "Are you the soda police?"

His look was stern. "I am until the nurse says you can have one."

"Ugh. Are you sure you love me? Love brings sodas," she pleaded.

"Love makes sure the nurse says sodas are okay. You get a soda when I hear the nurse okay a soda. There's a call button in your hand." He pointed at the device.

"Ugh! Meanie!"

"I accept my title. Call the nurse."

Carissa pushed the nurse call button on her hand control.

The nurse answered quickly. "Yes, ma'am. How can I help you?"

"My boyfriend says I have to ask you before he will go get me a soda. He's mean."

"Ha! Now that's a good boyfriend," the nurse told her. "You can have a clear soda. Nothing brown or any other color. Clear. You just came out of anesthesia. I don't want you to mess up your stomach. Clear soda," she repeated. "That's if you can figure out how to drink it lying down. Your doctor's orders say to keep you on your back for twenty-four hours but, if you can figure it out, you can have it." The nurse hung up.

"I want a Dr. Pepper," Carissa said.

"Great! Sprite it is. I'll be back," Isaac replied.

CHAPTER 31

Isaac went on his mission to find a soda. On his way out, he heard Carissa yell, "Mean! You're mean!" and he chuckled to himself. At least she felt well enough to argue.

At the end of the hallway, he found his pot of gold, a vending machine. He got himself some chips and a Sprite for Carissa. He also bought a Dr. Pepper for when she could have it.

He brought the loot back to the room, only to find Carissa sleeping. He decided not to disturb her, and left the Sprite on the table beside her while he took the chips and Dr. Pepper out to the waiting room where her parents were. He knew she'd sneak the Dr. Pepper if he left it there and, if the Dr. Pepper was off limits, he was sure the chips were, too.

In the waiting room, he found Mr. and Mrs. Schultz sitting in the same seats they had been in while they waited for Carissa to come out of surgery.

"How's she doing?" Jim asked.

"She's asleep." Isaac set the Dr. Pepper and chips on one of the tables close by. "She sent me on a soda mission, but couldn't hold out until I got back. Anesthesia is fighting her hard. She's losing the battle."

"Yeah," Jim commented, "she'll be in and out tonight. If you want to go home, I don't mind taking you. She'll be okay. You can drive back up tomorrow so you can have a car to come and go as you want to."

"If it's all right with you guys, I'd like to spend the night." Isaac stuffed his hands into his pockets. "I'll sleep out in the waiting room so I'm not sleeping in the room with her, if that makes you uncomfortable."

"You can stay as long as you'd like," Sarah said gently.

"If you need to go home at any point, though, just say the word," Jim put in. "It's no problem to run you back. And you can sleep where you're comfortable. She's not in any condition to do anything we wouldn't approve of. You can't get away with much," Jim replied, smiling indulgently.

"Yes, sir. I guess you're right," Isaac said. "Just trying to be respectful."

"I appreciate that." Jim leaned back in the waiting room chair.

They sat in the waiting room for a long while, letting Carissa rest. After some time, the receptionist came over.

"Are you guys with Carissa Schultz?"

"Yes, we're her mom and dad," Sarah answered.

"Well, her nurse asked me to let you know that she's fully awake now, and she'll be moving to a regular room soon," the woman said. "You may want to go back and find out where they'll be taking her."

"Thank you," Jim said.

They got up and headed back toward Carissa's room. "I assume we can all go back together, since they'll be moving her soon anyway. If not, well, we're doing it anyway!" he said as they walked down the hallway.

When they got to the room, they found Carissa with Sprite in hand, precariously drinking from a straw while lying flat and trying not to spill it on her face.

"Ha! Well, the nurse DID say you could have it if you could figure it out," Isaac laughed.

"I'm a pro," Carissa said around the straw. "Sorry I fell asleep."

"It's okay. You need to rest." Isaac touched her hand gently. "We have couch parties to get to."

"Yay, couch parties!" Carissa beamed at the thought. "As soon as they let me do something besides stare at the ceiling."

"I can wait," Isaac replied.

Then the nurse came in to take Carissa to the room where she'd stay for the remainder of her time in the hospital. Everyone followed down the hallway behind the big bed, Carissa still sipping on her Sprite.

An elevator and two floors later, they were settled into the room they'd be in until Carissa was released. The nurse came in and introduced himself. "Hi, I'm Chris. I'll be taking care of you for the rest of the day. If you need anything, you have a call button right here. Do you know how to use it?"

"Yeah, I kinda do this hospital thing," Carissa replied.

"Great! I see you have a Sprite. How's it doing on your stomach?" he asked, fussing with her pillows to make sure she was comfortable. "Are you nauseous or anything?"

"Nah, I'm fine," Carissa told him.

"Good deal. Do you think you could handle some crackers if I brought them?" Chris asked. "We want you to eat just a little bit tonight, and tomorrow we'll sit you up and make things easier.

Then you can have a full breakfast. Sound good?"

Carissa nodded. "Crackers sound okay. I'm not hungry. Still a little sleepy from everything. But I'll eat them if you bring them."

"Okay. I'll bring those. Let me know if you need anything else." Chris left to get her crackers.

CHAPTER 32

O ver the next couple of days, Carissa recovered well. She was eating, and she worked hard when physical therapy came.

By Sunday morning, Dr. Brock was looking at discharging. His opinion was that, if a person was able to recover at home, they should. It was an easier, more familiar environment. People did better in their own space. Carissa had improved to the point that he thought it best to let her do the rest of her healing at home.

He walked in the room that morning, and was met with a bright-eyed Carissa. She looked great for all she'd been through. "Hey, Carissa! What do you think of taking a car ride this afternoon?"

She looked up, surprised. "A car ride?"

"Maybe I wasn't clear. How would you like to go home?" he asked, grinning from ear to ear.

"I would love to go home!" She clapped her hands with delight.

"Well, I've looked at all your notes, and you're doing very well," he said with a smile. "I don't think there's anything we're doing here that you can't continue at home in a more comfortable environment. Unless you have some reason to want to hang out with me some more, I see no reason to keep you any longer. It'll just take some paperwork, and I can get you out the door. But you have to promise to keep up the rehab at home. Do your exercises. Don't go home and get stagnant on me. Work just as hard at home as you have here."

"I promise," she said.

"Well, then let me start that paperwork. I'll come let you know when you're free." Dr. Brock hurried out.

"Yes!" Carissa exclaimed. She wanted to be in her own home with fewer wake-up calls and less people in her face all the time. She wanted her own bed, and her couch, and her television, and less wake-up calls! Man, she was ready to get out of here.

"Looks like you're busting out in record time, kiddo!" Dad said.

"Couch party time!" exclaimed Isaac.

Sarah started packing up everyone's things. It was apparent that she wasn't staying there one minute longer than she had to. She'd emptied all the drawers in less than five minutes.

In another couple of hours, Dr. Brock popped his head in the door. "Hey, why aren't you dressed?" he joked. "I need this bed for another patient. Get out of here! You're free. Just sign these papers and take these documents with you when you go. These are your release papers," he handed her a single paper with a spot for a signature, "and these are your home instructions. Follow them. I'll know if you don't. I have eyes in the back of my head. Call my office as soon as you get home to schedule a follow-up in two weeks."

"Got it," Carissa said as she swiveled over to the side of the bed to slide on the sweat pants her mother handed her. "Isaac, Dad, privacy please," she said, and both men turned to face the wall.

Her mother helped her with the pants, since she was still sore and a little weak from surgery. She managed to get her shirt on by herself, and released Isaac and her dad from their wall prisons.

Jim and Isaac helped her into her chair, and they were on their way.

"Freedom!" Carissa called out as she wheeled down the hallways of the hospital. No one could blame her. She had worked hard to get out of the hospital so fast.

"I'll go ahead of you guys and bring the car around," Jim said. "You guys just wait at the front door if I'm not there when you get out."

"Great! Thanks, hon," Sarah replied.

Before long, they were all loaded into the car for the ride home. Carissa needed a little help, but she wasn't short of hands for the job.

The car ride home was much more upbeat than the car ride they'd taken a few days earlier. Carissa sang all the songs that came on the radio. Dad danced in the driver's seat. Sarah and Isaac were more reserved, but anyone could have seen their joy in being on their way home.

When they got there, no one bothered to make Carissa get back into her chair. Jim and Isaac carried her in, and Sarah brought the chair behind them. Inside, they set Carissa directly on the couch, where she had wanted to be since Friday.

"It's so good to be home," Carissa said, lying down and stroking the couch. It wasn't long before she fell asleep. She was doing well, but the car ride home and all the excitement had worn her out. Full recovery was still a long way off.

Jim, Sarah, and Isaac gathered in the kitchen so they wouldn't disturb her.

"Thank you so much for letting me be there for her," Isaac said. "I really appreciate it."

"Isaac, it was a very gentlemanly thing you did, to stay with her that long. We appreciate you more than you know. I believe you made her recovery easier just by being there," Jim replied.

"Yes, I definitely believe she did so well, at least in part, because you were there," Sarah confirmed.

"I wouldn't have wanted to be anywhere else," Isaac told them. "Hey, could one of you give me a ride home? I need to check on my mom. I've been in touch, and her nurse has stayed with her this whole time, but I still need to put eyes on her. You guys understand." When they nodded, he continued, "I kind of need a shower, too, and I have school tomorrow. I'd like to come back and spend the day with her after class, though, if that's okay."

"That's fine, Isaac. I'll take you home," Sarah replied.

After they left, Jim went to the living room to check on Carissa. She was still sleeping soundly, so he sat in the chair next to the couch and watched her. She had been through so much, but she always came through it beautifully.

Sometimes, Jim could tell she hated parts of the spina bifida, and she showed it but, even on her bad days, she still managed to power through. He was so proud of her. She was stronger than he could have imagined eighteen years ago, when he had held her tiny body for the first time.

CHAPTER 33

C arissa slept through the night, never moving from the couch. When she woke up, Isaac was already done with class and on the couch next to her.

"Hey," she mumbled.

"Hey, you!" Isaac grinned. "You hungry? I can make you something. I'm not a very good cook, though. You might not survive whatever I make, but you'll die full. Willing to risk it?"

She nodded. "I'll risk it."

"Glad to see you're getting back to your normal daredevil self. I think I can pull off a scrambled egg or two," he said. "Might even manage some cheese on top. Sound good?"

"Sounds perfect." Carissa laid her head back on her pillow.

"Good. Dr. Brock said he wanted you up and moving some, so why don't you come in the kitchen with me while I make it," he suggested. "Make sure I don't burn the house down."

"Ugh." Carissa moaned. She had not signed up for the getting-up part of this breakfast idea.

"Come on. Get up, lazy bones." Isaac wheeled her chair over. "No breakfast unless you travel for it."

She stuck out her tongue. "I'm calling the doctor. This is abuse."

"Okay. Call him. I'll call him. What's the number? Get up."

"You're mean," Carissa grumbled, sliding over into her chair so she could make her way to the kitchen.

Carissa noted that Isaac did his best to make decent scrambled eggs. "Mmm... looks good," she said. "Should I pray extra? Are you sure I won't die?"

He gave her a look. "I promise nothing."

"Eh... I'll risk just the one prayer then. I'm sure you didn't poison it."

"Not on purpose." He laughed aloud, the sound of pure delight.

Carissa scarfed the eggs in record time, and Isaac decided they were edible. Maybe it was all the cheese he'd put on top of the eggs.

"Where's my mom?" she asked between bites.

"I told her I'd keep an eye on you while she got a shower."

"Aw... boyfriend and babysitter!"

"You need no babysitter." He gave her a visual rebuke. "I'm making sure you don't decide you're healed and go off and do anything crazy."

"Someone should probably do that," she told him.

"How's your pain? Need a pill? You can have one since you ate."

"I could probably use one. I'm a little sore." Carissa hated to admit she still didn't feel her best, but it was what it was.

Isaac got up and went to the kitchen counter where Carissa's pills were, popped open the bottle, and brought one to her with a glass of orange juice.

"Thanks," she said, taking the pill and orange juice from him. "You're a good nurse."

"You're my most pleasant patient. You make my job easy."

"I do try and, by the way, I'm your only patient," Carissa replied.

Sarah walked into the kitchen.

"Hey, guys! Everything okay? I needed that shower. I feel refreshed now."

"We're good, Mom," Carissa responded.

"You take your meds?"

"Yep. All drugged up!" Carissa made a silly face, sticking out her tongue.

"Good," Sarah said. "Have you done your exercises?"

"Ugh. No. Mom, cut me some slack. I'm just barely awake," Carissa said.

"Slacking off already, I see." Sarah gave her daughter a reproving look. "Give your pain meds a few minutes to kick in, then get to it. Dr. Brock said not to get stagnant or you wouldn't heal. We want you to heal, don't we?"

"Not if it means moving."

"Yeah, well, it's not a choice," Sarah told her. "You have to heal. Mom said so."

"I'm eighteen. I can do what I want." Carissa leaned back against the cushions, arms resting in her lap.

"Good luck with that theory, living in your dad's house, kiddo! Rehab, then we can all pile on the couch for a movie. I'll make popcorn."

Carissa gave in grudgingly. "Ugh. All right."

She did her rehab for the day, which included some stretching and arm movements, followed by some rolling around the house to gain her strength and endurance back after being in bed for so long. As soon as she was done, she immediately transferred back to the couch and decided against moving again unless she was forced.

Isaac plopped down right beside her and put his arm around her. She slid over into his chest and found a comfortable spot for the movie. It wasn't long before she fell back asleep. Isaac was a good pillow, or rehab was exhausting, or both.

Weeks went on, and Carissa kept improving. Her post-op follow-up with Dr. Brock went perfectly. Unfortunately, she had missed too much school to go back for the semester, so she'd have to sit this one out. She hated having to miss a whole semester, but the surgery had been worth it. She hadn't even noticed how sick she'd felt before. Sometimes tethered cord came on gradually, Dr. Brock explained, and people didn't notice the changes happening in their bodies until things got pretty dramatic.

In Carissa's case, she only noticed the difference on the back end, after she recovered from surgery. She was able to move more, and her bladder was behaving better. She wasn't having as much pain as she had before.

Tonight, almost three weeks after surgery, she was going to Isaac's house to have dinner with him and his mother. She was nervous about driving over by herself, but felt recovered enough that it should be safe. Her mom and dad insisted she take her cell phone, and call if there were any problems. She should certainly call as soon as she arrived so they'd know she was safe.

CHAPTER 34

Jim and Sarah sat on their bed folding laundry. Sarah folded a towel and put it on the already leaning stack of towels she was working on.

"Are we sure she's good to drive?" Sarah asked. "I mean, I know the doctor cleared her for all activities, but are we sure? What if she starts to feel bad on the way?"

"Then she'll pull over and call, and I'll go get her," Jim said, and his calm tone reassured her. "She's fine, though. She's recovered well, and it's been three weeks. She says she feels better than before surgery. We can't keep her locked in the house forever. The only way she gets back to normal activities is to get back to them. That means we have to let her." He handed a dishcloth over and Sarah started a new stack.

"I know. I just worry. But if you think she's okay…"

"I know she's okay." He put his arm around her shoulders and squeezed. "We always worry, and she always proves us wrong.

Every time we think we have a reason to hold her back, she thrives. It's what she does. She'll be okay. And I know she knows what to do if she decides she's not okay."

"Okay. We let her go then." Sarah rearranged the towels and picked up a stack, getting up to put them in the master bathroom. She was still unsure, but was somewhat comforted by her husband's words.

"Bye, guys, I'm leaving, and I have my phone. I'll call as soon as I pull in Isaac's driveway!" Carissa shouted from the living room.

"Bye! We love you!" Sarah yelled back, heading back into the bedroom to sit next to Jim and fold more laundry.

And Carissa was on her first outing since surgery.

"See? Wasn't that easy?" Jim teased, poking Sarah lightly in the ribs.

"No," Sarah replied, swatting him off playfully.

"She'll be fine. We're watching from this end, and you know Isaac is on the lookout from his end. She's covered."

"Okay. I'll try to relax." But Sarah didn't sound very convincing. There weren't enough towels in the world to fold to keep her mind off letting Carissa go.

CHAPTER 35

Carissa called Isaac to let him know she was on her way. She didn't understand why everyone was so cautious. It wasn't like she had never driven before. But she still made sure to check in with everyone. It made them feel better, and whatever made them feel better about her getting out of that house was fine with her. She'd been cooped up too long. It was time to get back to life. If she couldn't go back to school, she was going to go somewhere, anywhere, to get off that couch.

So she headed to Isaac's couch. It had been a long time since she'd seen Betty, and she wanted to hear more stories about what it was like to fight for the ADA. She also had some questions for her about getting into the political scene. Carissa finally knew what her passion was, and she was ready to get started.

Carissa pulled up in Isaac's driveway and texted both of her parents, just to make sure at least one of them knew she had arrived safely. To her surprise, Isaac wasn't on the porch waiting for her. She got out of the car, rolled up to the door, and knocked.

Isaac came out in record time. Had he been standing there waiting? She wasn't going to ask. "I made it! No more disabled than I used to be, see?" She held out her arms. "Everyone can calm down. I'm alive and well."

Isaac reached down, put his arms around her and kissed her. "I'm glad you're safe. Dinner is almost ready. Mom is excited to see you."

"I'm excited to see her, too," Carissa replied. "We have a lot to talk about. It's been too long. Let's roll."

"You two," he said, walking beside her and holding the door open for her to go through. "I had a feeling you would find each other and be best friends, even if I didn't exist."

"Maybe, but you're definitely a bonus." She grinned back at him over her shoulder. "I like you a lot."

Carissa wheeled up to the table and settled in while Isaac helped his mom with the last of the dinner preparations. Soon, they both joined her, Isaac carrying a big pot of hearty stew, and Betty carrying a fresh-baked loaf of bread on her lap.

"I see the woman of the hour has arrived safely," Betty said. "How are you feeling, Carissa? Good? You look good! Did you let your parents know you got here safely? Don't want them worrying about you."

"I'm doing well, Ms.... Um... Betty." Would she ever get used to calling Isaac's mom by her first name? "Yes, I texted them both. Dinner smells awesome!"

Isaac had gone back to the kitchen and returned with a pitcher of lemonade. He walked around the table, pouring some into ice-filled glasses.

"Thanks, Isaac." Betty turned back to Carissa. "Beef stew," she said proudly. "My mama's recipe, and her mama's before that!

It's delicious. If you don't like it, I'll give you your money back, or this stinky boy, whichever you like!"

"I'm kind of fond of the stinky boy." Carissa shot Isaac an affectionate glance. "Can I have him and the stew?"

"We might be able to work something out." Betty laughed, a cheery mom-like laugh. It made Carissa feel almost like home.

"Good," she declared. "I like a good two-for-one deal."

"And that's why I like you." Betty reached over and patted Carissa's arm. "I like a woman who knows a good bargain when she sees one."

Isaac prayed over the meal, and everyone dug into the stew and bread. It was delicious, just as Betty had promised. Carissa and Betty talked like they had been best friends for years. Isaac mostly just ate.

"So, Betty, tell me more about what it was like to fight for the ADA. I mean, things aren't perfect, but that time in history sure made a lot of difference for people like us. I really want to know more." Carissa paused for a moment, her spoon hovering over her bowl. "I've been thinking," she said. "When I was in the hospital, I went for a stroll down to the nursery unit, and there was a baby there I could tell had spina bifida. I talked to his mom for a minute. That conversation lit a spark in me. I want to fight for babies like him. I want to fight for babies like me. Someone has to fight for people who can't fight for themselves, and I think I can do that. I want to do that."

"Well," Betty started, "it was hard. I'm not gonna lie to ya. People just didn't understand. Unless you have a disability, it's hard to understand what it's like to not be able to enter a place because it's inaccessible, or to not be able to get your chair into a bathroom stall when you really need to go, or even to be able to get around a shop when the aisle isn't big enough to get your chair through. Unless you've been in that situation, you just don't know."

Betty took a drink of the lemonade, resting her spoon on the bread plate next to her bowl. "So there was a lot of pushback, people saying all these laws were unnecessary, and we were just asking to be treated special. That wasn't true, though. We were just asking for equal opportunity, just to be able to be out in the world and struggle less. That's all we wanted, but we had to fight for it."

She gazed at Carissa intently. "Whatever's in that mind and heart of yours, I know you and I know it's good, but you're in for a fight. Nothing good comes without a strong fight. I can put you in touch with some of the people I fought next to. Maybe they can help you."

"I'd love that." Carissa reached out for Betty's hand, and felt the solidarity of it all. "It'll be nice to have people in my corner who already know the ropes. And I'm willing to fight for what's important to me, and for those babies."

"Good," Betty told her. "You need to keep that passion. It'll serve you well when you get tired… and you will get tired!"

They finished up dinner and, while Betty gathered some phone numbers and emails, Isaac and Carissa cleared the table and carried things into the kitchen. Isaac put the left-over stew in a plastic container and the bread in a Ziploc bag, and Carissa rinsed dishes and silverware and put them in the dishwasher.

Betty rolled back into the kitchen, carrying a piece of notebook paper. "Here's some contact information for people you can reach out to," she said, handing the paper to Carissa. "And now, I hate to run you off, but I'd better send you on home before it gets too late. I know your parents are being pretty cautious right now until you get on your feet a little better." She winked at Carissa. "You better get home to them before they start calling hospitals. Isaac, walk her out. You two can see each other tomorrow. And the next day. And the day after that. You know you will. Love birds. Carissa, we'll see you next time."

"Thanks so much." Carissa hugged Betty, truly appreciative of her efforts. "Bye, Betty. Thank you for the wonderful dinner, too."

"You give those people a shout," Betty told her. "Whatever you're up to, if it's in the disability rights realm, those are your people. They'll point you where you need to go."

"I'll get in touch with them," Carissa promised.

Isaac walked Carissa out. He stopped at the car door, opening it so she could move from her chair into the driver's seat. Leaning down, he said, "I don't know what you're up to, but I'm excited for you. Whatever this is, I want to be with you when you accomplish it."

"Just saving the world. No big deal," she replied.

"Sounds like a big deal to me." He put her chair into the passenger side, then came around and kissed her.

"Well, maybe it will be someday." She returned the kiss, then smiled up at him. "Your support is much appreciated."

Carissa went home with a fire in her heart, excited for what the future might hold. Surgery recovery had been long and hard, but she finally felt like her head and heart were back in the game. It was time to get this thing moving. It was time to change the world, if only her tiny corner of it. Seeing that baby, and talking with his mother, had changed something inside her. She could never unknow what she knew now, and she had to do something about it. Maybe the people Betty told her about could help.

When she pulled into her driveway, she texted Isaac to let him know she was home safe. "I'm home. Loved dinner. Thank you both." She got out of the car, rolled up the sidewalk, and went into the house.

"Hi," she called. "I'm home!"

"We're in the bedroom," Sarah answered, "watching one of your dad's infamous movie picks."

"Okay," Carissa said. "I'm going to get ready for bed."

She went to her room. It was too late to make any phone calls, but she could email some of the people Betty had told her about. She started at the top of the list, and worked her way down, telling everyone on the list about the ideas she had. She didn't even know how to get into politics. That was why she had gone pre-law in the first place, to learn her way around the system. For now, though, school was on hold, and she had to find another way in. She volunteered for politicians. She asked to be allowed to attend meetings, and she asked for anyone to volunteer to hear her heart.

Finally, she shut down her laptop and prayed. "God, I feel You talking. I feel Your pull. That boy in the nursery... I heard his story, and it changed me. No human life should ever be treated the way he was treated. Use me to make sure it doesn't happen again."

* * *

When Carissa had been in the hospital, she had run into the tiny baby and his mother during a rehabilitation session, wheeling around the hospital for endurance. She had stopped to look at the babies and seen him in his incubator. She could tell he had spina bifida by the way the gauze was wrapped around his back lesion. His mother had come out of the nursery at about the same time Carissa spotted him.

She gazed down at Carissa in her chair. "You know," she said, "they say my boy will be in a wheelchair, too. I don't know what to expect. My doctor encouraged me to abort every time I went in for a check-up." Tears started running down her face, and her eyes took on a haunted look. Carissa reached for the woman's hand and held onto it.

"But you didn't," she said softly.

"I couldn't do that to my baby," the woman said. "I told her I wouldn't do it. She just kept pushing. It was like she thought his life wasn't worth living, almost like he was a piece of garbage that needed to be thrown out. She just kept pressuring and pressuring. Told me and my husband this wasn't what we wanted, that we could start over with a new, healthy baby. That it would be easier. That he would never walk, talk, or feed himself. That he'd be dependent on us for everything, if he even lived at all."

She sobbed, her shoulders shaking by the force of her emotion. "But this was my boy! I couldn't do it. I don't know what happens from here, but I know I want THIS baby. I would never have aborted him. That's my son. I wish that doctor could see him now, my boy. He's a beautiful baby. I wish she could just see." The mother turned toward the nursery window, love pouring from her.

"He has spina bifida?" Carissa asked.

"Yes. They aren't sure what he'll be capable of yet. All the doctors here say it's just wait and see, but the prognosis is so much better than my doctor gave. They say he will likely be of normal intelligence, that eating may be a challenge, based on some other complications he could have, but that he'll probably be able to do it. Walking is up in the air. They say he'll just have to show us." She looked back to Carissa, and smiled through her tears. "But it's so much better than what we thought. So much better. I'm so glad I didn't abort him. He's so beautiful."

"He really is," Carissa replied. "What did you name him?"

"Christopher," the mother said. "I just wish my doctor had told me the truth. I'm not even sure she knew the truth. She acted like my baby was some sort of mutant. Like he wouldn't be normal. Like he wasn't even a baby. I thought I was giving birth to a monster, but look at him. He's just a little boy. He has some challenges, but we'll deal with them. That's my boy in there."

Carissa shook her head. "It's hard for me to believe they're still telling parents all that stuff. I have friends with spina bifida whose parents were all told the same things. Some of them walk; some of them don't." She smiled up at this mother, knowing she was confused and full of questions. "But we're all pretty independent and normal, outside of that. I understand why they said it about us. They just didn't know what we could do, and things looked pretty bad back then. There wasn't all the same medical technology, and I just don't understand why they're still saying that when my generation has clearly proven it false. I'm so sorry you went through that. I wish you'd been told the truth from the beginning."

The other woman agreed. "I do, too. It would have made my pregnancy much easier. I was sure I was carrying a dying baby inside me. It was so scary. But look at him. He's really okay!"

"Yes, he's really okay," Carissa reassured her. "This is a good life. I just want you to know that. I know you're probably still scared of how he'll do in the world, but it's good on this side, chair or not. He'll be fine."

"Thank you." Christopher's mother leaned down and hugged Carissa. "Thank you so much."

* * *

Carissa left that conversation feeling angry and helpless, but maybe there was something she could do. She was just one person, but she still had a voice. That little baby in there didn't, and she knew there were thousands more babies like him who also needed a voice to speak for them.

She wasn't sure how she'd do it, but she had to do something. What she heard could not be unheard. That beautiful boy could not be unseen. Once she was sure she could do no more tonight, she climbed into bed and texted Isaac. "Turning in now. I love you and goodnight."

"Okay. Goodnight, I love you, too," he texted back.

She snuggled down in her pillow. She was so happy with Isaac, but not happy about those children like Christopher. But she'd find a way to make things better, with God's help and the help of anyone else who wanted to join her on her quest.

CHAPTER 36

Annabelle Jenkins started her work day by checking her email. She deleted almost every one as spam, or some over-zealous idiot text-screaming at her about things she had no control over. She loved the citizens of her state, but sometimes they got a little rowdy for her. After all, she wasn't the governor. She was only an assistant in his office. She had no power. She didn't know what they expected her to do about their concerns. If the governor wasn't doing what they thought he should be doing, they should email him. That's why his email address was public. She didn't have the power or the time to do anything about their complaints, especially with the amount of paperwork the governor put on her desk every day. She had complaints of her own.

She got to the very last email in her inbox, and almost deleted it, too, until she read the word "Spina Bifida" in the title. Her five-year-old daughter Isabella had spina bifida. When Annabelle was pregnant, the doctors told her all the horrible things that would happen to her unborn child. She'd never walk. She'd be mentally retarded. She'd be incapable of a normal life. They had pushed her to abort and, with all the pressure and such a bad prognosis, she almost had. But she hadn't, and it was the best decision of her life.

Her daughter had exceeded all expectations. She walked, did all of her own self-care except putting on her leg braces. They were working on that issue, and Isabella would enter kindergarten this year in a normal classroom. So much for that bad prognosis. Her girl had taken those words and tossed them in the garbage!

Annabelle opened the email, and what she found inside both saddened and excited her. Carissa was a young woman born with spina bifida, and it looked like she was passionate about making some real change. Now this, Annabelle could get behind. She re-read the email.

Dear Ms. Jenkins,

I am a young woman born in the '90s with myelomeningocele spina bifida. I'm a friend of Betty Carter, who you worked with to start the Americans with Disabilities Act in the 1980s.

First of all, I would like to thank you for all the work you did back then to make it easier for those of us born in this generation to navigate the world. I'm sure the disabled before my generation did not have it as easy, so thank you. I don't know if you're disabled or not, but you sure had a hand in making my life less challenging than it might have been.

I wanted to talk about playing my part in disability rights. I believe it's time for my generation to take over the torch and make what you did even stronger and better. I believe we can go further in protecting our rights as people, but I need some help. I want to make sure that doctors who are giving out a diagnosis of lifelong disability are required to tell the honest, full truth about the disability they are diagnosing. It is my belief that many babies are needlessly killed based on disability, when the prognosis for that particular child is simply untrue, due to lack of physician knowledge and education. It is my understanding that physicians are handing out a prognosis based on literature that was written as far back as the 1950s. Medical research has come too far to rely on those sources to predict accurate futures for these children.

Doctors are still handing out the same bleak prognosis that was handed to my parents when I was born, and it wasn't true or accurate even then. Babies are losing their lives over false information. This isn't a pro-life or pro-choice issue. This is a truth issue.

Doctors should be required to keep themselves up to date on the latest research and treatments these babies are receiving if there is any chance they'll be handing out this type of diagnosis. They should be held to a higher standard of education and knowledge, starting with the textbooks they learn from in school and continuing on throughout their whole careers. No family should have to face the idea of aborting their child because of false information.

In fact, no parent should be offered an abortion based on a false prognosis. It should be illegal to offer an abortion before having all of the current medical statistics on hand and ready to show these mothers and fathers. I don't believe in abortion at all, but abortion based on false evidence of disability is a whole other playing field. It's wrong and unfair to both the parents and the babies. Parents deserve the truth, and these babies deserve it too. Please help me help them.

Sincerely,
Carissa Schultz

Annabelle Jenkins put her head down on her desk, almost in tears. This had happened to her and her baby, too. She almost lost her sweet girl, not because she wanted to abort, but because the picture painted for her had been so bleak that she thought she might have no other choice. She thought the only choice she had as a good mother was to let her child stop suffering. She was so glad she hadn't had the strength to go through with the abortion. To see her daughter now, she saw no suffering. She saw a little girl conquering. She had to help Carissa.

She picked up the phone and called the only person she could think of, Connie Peterson. Connie was the leader of a statewide spina bifida parents' support group. They met in chapters once a month to have a meal and discuss issues, and sometimes just to feel like normal parents. In a group of moms and dads facing the same things you faced every day, sometimes the stigma of raising a disabled child got pushed to the back burner. Her local chapter was Annabelle's lifeline. If anyone could gather the numbers together to make this happen, it was Connie. Connie could get this done.

The phone rang three times before Connie picked up. "This is Connie Peterson. How can I help you?"

"Connie! Hey, this is Annabelle, out of the southeast Texas chapter. I got an email this morning that I think might interest you. A young woman with spina bifida has a fire lit under her butt and wants doctors to tell the truth about spina bifida and other birth defects. Imagine that! Doctors finally telling the truth. Can I forward you the email? If anyone can get enough heads together to help this girl out, it would be you."

"Annabelle, you think too highly of me, but send the email on. I'll take a look."

"Thank you!" Annabelle said. "You're the best."

Connie laughed out loud. "I am the best. That's why you called me, right?"

"You know it. Bye, Connie!"

Annabelle hung up the phone and forwarded the email, then emailed Carissa back, telling her what the plan was.

CHAPTER 37

C arissa woke up early the next morning, eager to check her email. She knew it was a long shot, but she hoped she had grabbed the heartstrings of someone out there who could help her. She popped out of bed, opened up the laptop on her desk, and logged on. There was an email from one of the people on Betty's list, Annabelle Jenkins.

"Oh, wow. This could be it. Or, you know, it could be one of those stock emails, saying 'Thank you for emailing. We don't care. Vote for us next year!' or something worse," Carissa told herself, trying unsuccessfully not to get too excited. She clicked the email to open it.

Dear Ms. Schultz,

Thank you so much for inquiring about this matter. I have a daughter born with spina bifida myself, so your cause is near and dear to my heart. I think I may be able to help you. I've forwarded your email to Connie Peterson, who leads a state-wide support group for parents of children with spina bifida. If she sees fit, she will forward your email and ideas to all the local chapters of her group. If anyone can get the ball rolling, she can. She can gather enough bodies to make Congress hear us, and I, for one, plan to be one of those bodies. I look forward to working with you on this.

– Annabelle Jenkins

Carissa's heart pounded. She had done it! Someone had listened to her. God had made a way. Nothing was impossible with God. What were the chances that the person on the other side of that email address had a daughter born with spina bifida? This was big stuff. Carissa could feel it. Something big was coming, but all she could do for now was wait to hear from this Connie person. She hoped Connie would be on board.

She signed out of her email and went out to see if Mom had anything for breakfast. She was not disappointed.

"Hey, honey, want some scrambled eggs and sausage?" Sarah asked, looking up from the stove.

"Do I? Of course I do! Have I ever rejected sausage? Ever?" Carissa asked.

"Not since you grew teeth," Sarah replied. She brought a skillet full of eggs and sausage over to the table, scooped Carissa some, and then helped herself. Setting the skillet back on the stove, she poured two cups of coffee and carried them to the table, giving one to Carissa and putting the other one next to her own plate.

"So what's up, kid? You seem perky for so early in the morning. Last night go well with Isaac and Betty?"

"Mom, you have no idea. I think I'm onto something big."

Carissa added sugar and cream to her cup. "See, Ms. Carter used to work with the same people that got the ADA started, back in the eighties. She was kind of a big deal in it, even before she got injured in the car accident. She was one of the ones who made it all happen."

"Very cool!" Sarah replied. "So you guys talked about that?"

"Yeah, and Mom, I have an idea." Excitement beamed out from her face. "Knowing Betty did it, I think it's time for my generation to step up. You know I've had law school on my heart for a while, wanting to change things for people with spina bifida, right?"

"Right..." Sarah waited, feeling Carissa's energy.

"Well," Carissa said, her voice fiery at the thought of the challenge, "I can't go back right now, but I think I found my REAL passion... the babies, the ones who don't have a voice and can't fight for themselves."

"Okay..." Sarah waited for more.

Carissa continued on, her body animated. "I wrote an email to one of Betty's friends from the ADA fight. Well, actually, I wrote several emails, but only one person replied. She wants to help me. I think I can do this."

"What? You think you can do what with babies? What are we so excited about, hon? I want to be excited, too, but I'm feeling more nervous than excited right now." Sarah rested her elbows on the table, a bit overwhelmed. "Perhaps let me in on your project, so I don't start coming up with ways to find bail money."

"Mom, remember when you were pregnant, and the doctors told you I wouldn't live? And, if I did live, I'd have all these horrible complications? And how you might be better off not having me at all because, even if I lived, I'd be miserable?" Carissa took a big swallow of her doctored-up coffee and leaned back in her chair, not noticing that her nice, warm breakfast was cooling.

"I'll never forget," Sarah admitted.

"It wasn't true then," Carissa stated.

"No, it wasn't."

Carissa rushed on. "Well, I met a woman when I was in the hospital. Her baby has spina bifida, and they told her all the same things! It wasn't true then, and it's definitely not true now, but they're still saying it. Doctors are still getting their information out of the same outdated textbooks they were when you were pregnant, and new moms and dads have to make life-and-death decisions based on that outdated information."

Carissa's enthusiasm for her cause captured Sarah's attention. Carissa continued. "Babies who are perfectly capable of living long, happy, healthy lives, are dying due to false, outdated information, but I think we can do something about it. We can make these doctors educate themselves. We can make it a law that no prognosis can be handed out without the doctor getting all the latest research, not just telling parents what he read out of a fifty-year-old textbook when he was in med school. It's only fair that parents get the truth. You know I don't believe in abortion at all but, if I can only save a few, I want to save them."

"Sweetheart, I'm really excited for you, but this is BIG. I'm not sure you understand how big this could get. You'll get a lot of pushback. It might get really emotional and overwhelming for you. Or it might never take flight." Sarah gave her daughter a penetrating look. "Are you sure you can handle it if this idea of yours never leaves the ground? Are you sure you have to be the one? What if this takes over so much of your life that you can't get back to school next semester? You're only eighteen. This is a lot to take on."

"I have to be the one, Mom. No one else is doing it. This is important to me." Carissa reached across the table and took her mom's warm hand. "It's already overwhelming me," she said, "but not for the reasons you think. It's overwhelming me because I can't sit here another minute knowing what I know and not doing anything about it. I can't let babies die, knowing I could say something and it would all stop."

Her eyes pleaded with Sarah. "It's already emotional for me, Mom. I AM one of those babies. You and Dad could have chosen differently. The only difference between me and them is that you and Dad chose to keep me despite all the horrible things the doctors told you. It IS emotional, but I have to do it. And, even if the idea never takes off, I have to know I tried."

"Okay, hon," Sarah smiled encouragingly, "then I'm behind you. This is big, though. It's a lot to handle."

"I know, Mom, but I don't have any other choice. I can't live with myself if I don't try."

"Then you have to," Sarah smiled, tears glistening in her eyes, "and I'll support you. I love you, kid."

"Love you, too, Mom."

Sarah picked up their still-full plates and placed them in the microwave for a quick warm-up, then she and Carissa finished breakfast and put the dishes in the dishwasher.

Carissa hugged Sarah, then went to her room to do some research on her new project. She needed to be able to present her case with facts, not just emotion. She was hard at work, deep into cyberspace, when her email alert dinged. She recognized the name in the address bar immediately. Connie Peterson. This was everything, or nothing. She opened it up.

Carissa,

I have received the email you sent to Ms. Jenkins, and I

have to say, I'm absolutely on board with helping you. You're right. At the very least, parents facing spina bifida, or any other birth defect, should be given correct information before being given the option to abort. Let me talk to the leaders of our support group. I'll let them toss some ideas back and forth, and we'll come up with a plan for how to get this law written and looked at. I'm excited for what this might bring about. You'll hear from me again soon.

– Connie Peterson

Carissa took in a deep breath. Ms. Jenkins had told her that, if anyone could help, it would be Connie, and it looked like Connie was all in. This might actually become something.

CHAPTER 38

C onnie Peterson drew in a long breath and remembered the day her son was born. Tears began to fill her eyes as she recalled the horrible things the doctor told her. He'd never walk. He'd never talk. He'd be fully dependent on her for the rest of his life, and that life would be a short one. He was twenty-five now. He was married, independent and, though not without struggle, he and his wife were expecting their first baby soon.

Connie knew she had to help Carissa. She knew the same things she'd been told about her son were still being said today, and something had to be done. What they had told her wasn't true twenty-five years ago, and it wasn't true now. It was time that doctors caught up with medical technology and started handing out more realistic outlooks for these children. These parents and children deserved the truth. Connie opened up her long list of email addresses for all the individual leaders of each local support group chapter, and began to type a group email.

Ladies and Gentlemen,

I received an email today that both broke my heart and
called me to action. I have attached a copy of it to this cor-
respondence. I believe you will be on board with this young
lady once you read what she wrote. I believe the story she
tells is one that will be very familiar to most of you. Please
share it with your local chapters and let's help her get the
ball rolling on this. I feel like it is past time to do something
about this issue, and that we are the right people to handle
it. I look forward to hearing back from each of you soon.

– Connie Peterson

Connie hit the send button and tried to move onto other things.
She couldn't wait to hear back from the leaders, but it would be
days at least, depending on what day each individual chapter had
its weekly meeting. This was exciting stuff, and she felt honored
to be a part of it. She called her son John to let him know what was
going on, and he was excited to get in on it, too.

"Hello?" Connie heard John pick up on the other end of the
line.

"Hey, son, you'll never guess what I'm up to! I think you'll be
excited."

"What's up?" he replied, sounding curious.

"Well, I received an email. You know Annabelle, with the little
girl, Isabella, who has spina bifida?"

"Yeah…"

Connie couldn't hold in her excitement. She took a long drink
of her coffee and stood up from her desk, starting to pace. "Well,
she received an email today from a young woman named Carissa
who has spina bifida, too. Carissa is interested in taking a law to

the Capitol that would change everything for babies with spina bi-fida. She wants to make doctors actually research current medical advancements before giving a prenatal diagnosis to new parents."

She paused to take quick sip of coffee. "They'd have to learn about the latest medical technology and how it's helping before handing out a prognosis. It wouldn't be the doom-and-gloom scenario that was handed to me and so many other parents. She wants these doctors to have to arm themselves with the truth. A true, up-to-date prognosis for these babies, handed out right from the start. What a difference it would make! How much hope would it give?" Connie finally sat back down at her desk, having unloaded all of her excitement into the phone.

"That's amazing!" John exclaimed. "I'm in for helping. Let me know what I can do." Connie heard the sincerity in his voice.

"Okay, I will. For now, son, just pray," she said.

"I'm on it! I love you, Mom. Keep me informed."

"I love you, too." Connie hung up the phone and again tried to occupy her mind with something other than Carissa and her cause.

CHAPTER 39

Waiting for Isaac to pick her up for their dinner date, Carissa sat in the white wooden rocker on her front porch, too excited to stay in the house.

He had called earlier in the week and invited her out, and she couldn't wait to tell him in person about the emails she'd exchanged with Annabelle and Connie. She knew he'd be excited, too. She only wished she could tell Betty at the same time, but that could wait. This night was for Isaac and her.

She saw him pull around the corner onto her street, her excitement threatening to bubble over. He turned into the driveway, getting out to help her with her chair, and she got into the front passenger seat.

"Hey, I've missed you," he said, lifting her chair into the car.

"I've missed you, too," she replied. "Where's dinner?"

"I thought we'd try that Italian place by the mall," he grinned. "You into that?"

She nodded enthusiastically. "I'm into anything with tomatoes and garlic!"

"That's my girl!" He climbed into the driver's seat, started the car, and shifted into drive.

As they headed toward the restaurant, Carissa sang every song that played on the radio. She wasn't normally comfortable singing with other people around, but there was something comfortable about Isaac. She could be her goofy self around him and not care that he saw the real her. She snuggled into that secure feeling. "I have something to tell you, but you have to wait until we get to the restaurant," she told him.

"Uh, oh..." he replied, jokingly.

"It's not bad!" she assured him. "But I'm not telling until we get there because I'm too excited. It has to be a face-to-face conversation, not a car trip talk."

"Okay!" He glanced over at her with a big grin. "If you're excited, I'm excited!"

They pulled into the restaurant parking lot, and Isaac got Carissa's chair, setting it next to the open door for her. She slid into the seat and they went inside. There was a short wait, but it wasn't long before they were seated. Carissa was glad for the promptness; she'd almost blurted out her secret before she wanted to.

"Okay, what do you have to tell me?" Isaac asked, sliding into the chair opposite her. If she was excited about something, he wanted to be in on it.

"Oh, gosh," she said, "you know how I've been saying I want to change things for people with spina bifida, right?"

"Yep. Got that," he replied. It was one of the first things he'd learned about her, that she wanted to change things for people like her. He'd fallen in love with her passion for making the world better.

"Okay, so I've been thinking." She leaned across the table, her eyes bright with intensity. "Who are the most vulnerable people like me? Babies, right?"

"Um… I don't think we've been dating long enough to be talking about babies," he joked.

"No, you goof! Not OUR babies! Babies with spina bifida!"

"Oh," he laughed. "Okay. I'm back in."

She continued, serious now. "Well, when I was born, my parents were told a lot of awful things about me that weren't true. You know that. I've told you how they said I wouldn't live, and I'd be mentally challenged and all that if I did live."

"Yeah." He nodded.

"Well, those things are still being said today about unborn babies. Doctors are handing out false, outdated information and, in a lot of cases, parents are choosing abortion based on that information."

Isaac waited, listening for what she wanted to say.

"Well," she said, "I've decided to do something about it. I wrote to all the people your mom put me in contact with and one emailed me back this week. Her name is Annabelle Jenkins. She has a daughter with spina bifida, and her daughter's story matches my story. Annabelle's an assistant of some sort in the governor's office, and she's on board for helping me make a law. She forwarded my email to a friend of hers, who is apparently a big shot leader of a spina bifida support group. That means lots of support and voices for the cause. Isaac, this could get big. I really could be about to change things!"

Isaac was astonished. He knew Carissa was a firecracker, but he didn't see all of this coming. "I'm so proud of you! How can I help? When will you know when and how to take the next steps?"

"I don't know. Connie said she'd get back to me when she

heard back from the leaders of each individual chapter of the support group, so I guess we just wait for now."

"Then I'll wait with you. This is exciting! You're gonna be famous," he said, her enthusiasm firing him up.

"Okay, calm down. I don't know about famous," Carissa replied.

"My girlfriend is going to be famous," Isaac told the waitress as she came to get their drink orders.

"Is that so?" the waitress asked, joking back with him. "Well, what would you like to drink then, ma'am? I wouldn't want to disappoint future fame!"

"Coke is fine, and my boyfriend is crazy! Ignore him," Carissa replied.

"Aren't they all? And what can I get for you to drink, sir?" she asked.

"Coke is fine with me as well, thank you," Isaac said.

The waitress went to get their Cokes.

"It's too bad we're not older," Isaac told Carissa. "This is really more a wine occasion than a Coke occasion, but Coke will have to do."

Carissa laughed. "Coke is perfect."

They ordered their food, lasagna and salad, and dreamed out loud about the day Carissa would be able to get her law passed. Isaac promised to be there with her every step of the way.

"You make me happy," he said, putting a forkful of noodles, beef and sauce into his mouth, "and anything that makes you happy, I'm into it."

They finished their meal, each of them stealing bites off the other's plate, and finally decided it was time to leave the almost empty restaurant before they got kicked out.

Isaac paid the bill, and they exited into the warm night.

"Do you want to go sit on the beach?" he asked.

"Um... well... my chair... it doesn't maneuver on sand too well."

"Let me worry about that. Do you want to go?" he repeated.

"Sure, I guess, if you think you can handle it, macho man!" She loved his spontaneity and fun spirit.

"I've got this!" he yelped. "You just get in the car!"

"Yes, sir, whatever you say!" she replied, unsure if he knew what he was getting himself into.

She had gone to the beach once when she was little. Her chair sank down into the sand immediately, and she hadn't been able to propel anywhere. Her parents ended up carrying her the whole day. It wasn't fun for anyone. She loved the water, though, and the sound of the waves. She just hoped Isaac understood that the beach was not built with people like her in mind. She got in the car, however, and they made their way down to Galveston Island.

When they arrived, Isaac parked the car on the sand overlooking the water. The moon made light crystals on top of each tiny wave. Isaac came around to get Carissa, but left her chair in the back seat.

"Hey, my wheels!" she protested.

"I'm your legs tonight," he said, gently lifting her out of the car. Then he took her just to the edge of the water and sat her down in the sand.

"It's beautiful out here," Carissa said.

"I know. Everyone should experience it," he agreed.

They sat in the sand for a long time, building castles. Isaac, at one point, started on a different shape.

"What are you making?" Carissa asked. "That's not like any castle I've ever seen."

"Texas snowman," Isaac replied.

"A what?"

"Texas snowman." He grinned mischievously. "You've never heard of it? I mean, we don't get snow, so... this is our version. You need to get to the beach more. You've been deprived of a true Texas tradition."

Carissa laughed at him and threw a small handful of sand his direction. "You're such a goof! That's not a real snowman."

"Hold on tight!" he yelled at her, scooping her up, running toward the water.

"I can't swim," she cried.

"That's what you get for making fun of my snowman!"

"My clothes!" she half-yelled, half-giggled at him.

"Oh, well, my snowman didn't deserve that. You're going in!"

"But I really can't swim!" she yelled, sounding more concerned than before.

"I've got you. I won't let go. I won't let anything happen to you, unless a shark comes!" He laughed back at her.

"ISAAC!" she yelled.

"I've got you, see?" he reassured her, squeezing her tighter into him. "You're okay. I won't let anything happen. Just hold onto me." They stayed in the water for a long time. Carissa realized she felt free to move more in the water than she ever had anywhere else. It was nice to be able to move like that. It was also nice to be held by Isaac while she did.

"I love you," she told him. "And I'm sorry I made fun of your snowman. Sort of."

"You know, I don't have to bring you back to shore," he joked with her.

"You would never leave me here."

He grinned down at her. "Do you feel lucky?"

"No, I feel loved."

"You are loved," and he kissed her gently, then brought her back to land.

It was getting late, so the two of them decided it was time to end the night and head back home. Isaac carried Carissa back to the car and turned the heater on so she wouldn't be cold in her wet clothes.

"I didn't bring towels. I wasn't really planning to go in the water," Isaac said.

"It's okay. I don't melt in water. It dries eventually," Carissa responded.

They took the long drive off the island and back to Carissa's house, and Isaac walked her up to the door.

"Goodnight. I had fun tonight," Carissa told him.

"I'm glad," he responded, kissing her goodnight.

Carissa went into the house and headed straight to her bathroom to shower and get her pajamas on, trying to avoid any weird eyes from her parents. Her clothes had only half-dried from the ocean, and she still smelled like salt water. In the shower, she remembered the feeling of weightlessness and freedom the ocean had brought. She also remembered Isaac's arms around her, and how protected she felt. It was incredible.

CHAPTER 40

Connie Peterson got to the office early Monday morning and began checking emails. Along with the regular concerns of the support group, she had four emails in response to the one she had sent regarding Carissa. All of them wanted to hear more about what Carissa was hoping to accomplish and how they could help. Two group leaders sent back their own personal stories that matched the story of Carissa's parents, along with confirming that there were several more similar stories in their local chapters.

It was starting to look like this was a bigger problem than Connie thought, and these stories were only coming from parents who had chosen to give their children life despite the terrible prognosis. How many moms and dads had actually gone through with the abortions based on such information? She would probably never know.

She decided to email Annabelle and Carissa to let them know what was going on. They'd be excited to hear of the support. First, though, Connie needed fuel. She stepped over to the coffee pot and put some on to brew. She made it strong this morning. She would need a lot of energy to get this ball rolling. When it was done, she poured herself a cup, black, and sat down to write the first email.

Dear Carissa and Annabelle,

You'll be excited to hear that I've received several responses back from the email I sent regarding the law we've been talking about. This problem seems to be widespread in our community, and I suspect we'll never know how far it truly reaches. Many parents probably take the information given to them as truthful and choose to abort, and we may never know how many fall into that category. Everyone who has responded so far, though, seems interested in getting the ball rolling in this area, and I expect to hear from more this week. Carissa, for eighteen years old, you sure are a mature young lady. I suspect you'll take this far. Annabelle, maybe you could give us some insight into how we get this to Austin? I look forward to hearing back from you both, and can't wait to be behind you in this endeavor.

– Connie Peterson

She sent the email off and got to work responding to the rest that had come in over the weekend. It took her most of the day to respond to everyone who was interested in helping Carissa with her idea. There would be no shortage of boots, or wheels, on the ground for this.

CHAPTER 41

C arissa woke up early Monday morning. She got out of bed and cracked open her laptop to check her email. In it was an email from Connie Peterson, the leader of the spina bifida support group that Carissa hoped would get behind her on the law she wanted passed. She took a deep breath and clicked it open.

She couldn't believe what she read. Connie already had full support from four different chapters of the support group, and she expected more support to come. Carissa clicked to close Connie's email and realized she had several more from addresses she didn't recognize.

She opened them one by one and, in each, found a story of either a parent of a child with spina bifida or an adult with spina bifida who heard her story at a support group meeting and wanted to get behind her. All of their stories matched hers. It was unbelievable. There must have been thirty separate stories of families all given the wrong prognosis, and it was only Monday. Most of the chapters of the support group hadn't even met yet.

Carissa tried to respond to each email with thanks, but there were just too many to get to right away. She shut down her laptop, deciding she would come back later to reply to the rest. She needed some breakfast, and she needed to tell her mom everything that was happening.

"Hey, you!" Sarah called out as Carissa rolled into the kitchen.

"Hey!" Carissa replied, grabbing the coffee pot and pouring herself a cup.

"How was your date the other night?" Sarah asked. "You were out kinda late. Haven't seen much of you since then."

"It was great! We had Italian and went to the beach. We left my chair in the car and he carried me."

"Nice!" Sarah exclaimed. "Want breakfast? Just pancakes this morning."

"Just pancakes? Wow, you know that's my favorite breakfast," Carissa said.

"Comin' up." Sarah went to the stove and heated up a skillet, then poured pancake batter into the pan.

"It was so nice," Carissa told her. "But, Mom, guess what else? Guess!"

"I don't know!" Sarah flipped the pancakes over, then carried butter and syrup to the table. "Don't have a clue. What else?"

"So, you know I've been working with Annabelle Jenkins on this thing about getting doctors to tell the truth about babies with spina bifida, right?"

"Right." Sarah walked back over to the stove, lifted the pancakes onto a plate, and brought them over and set the plate in front of Carissa.

"Thanks, Mom," Carissa said, smiling up at her mom. "Well, I heard back from Connie Peterson, the lady over that statewide spina bifida support group. Just over the weekend, four of the chapters of the group decided to get behind us on getting a law passed. And it's only Monday!" Carissa took a breath and forked a bite of pancake into her mouth. "Umm," she commented on her breakfast, then continued. "Most of the groups haven't even met yet, so this is huge! And, Mom, families are emailing me personally to say they've had the same experience, and they're behind me and want to help."

"That IS huge!" Sarah replied. "So what's the next step? What do we do to make this happen?"

"We wait," Carissa sighed. "Annabelle Jenkins is supposed to give us our next steps. All we can do right now is wait and pray."

"Well, then, that's what we'll do," Sarah said firmly. "We'll wait and pray. Your dad is going to be so excited! You should tell him as soon as he gets home."

"I will," Carissa said, wondering how her mom might think she wouldn't tell her dad what was going on as soon as he walked in the door.

As promised, Carissa told the exciting news as soon as he got home from work. Sarah had cooked a pot roast and had everything waiting for dinner. As soon as the blessing was said, Carissa filled him in on the progress of her new project, her excitement contagious.

"That's great, honey!" Jim said when she finished telling him everything that had happened. "Let me know when I can help. I'm totally behind you on this."

She smiled. He always was behind her, in her corner, ready to help. "Just pray for now, Dad. I'm kind of just waiting for everything to get set in place."

"Good enough for me," he told her. "Your mom and I will be sure to pray."

"Thanks, Dad!"

They finished dinner and Carissa helped clear the table, then went to her room to call Isaac. Before she could tell him the big news, he chimed in with news of his own.

"Hey!" he exclaimed. "I've been waiting to hear from you. I have big stuff!"

"Me, too, but you go first," she replied.

"Okay. If you're sure…" he hesitated.

"I'm sure; go ahead, I want to hear your news. Mine can wait."

"Okay, so you know how I've been working at the library part-time…" he started.

"Yeah." She remembered the first time she'd seen him there, so long ago. They'd been through a lot since then.

"Well, I've been kind of fishing around here and there, looking for something more in the medical field, and I landed something! I start in the medical center on Wednesday. It's daytime, only paper pushing for now, but they say as I complete school, I might be able to move up. And they'll even allow me to come in a little bit late for the rest of this semester so I can finish up these classes."

He took a breath. "Of course," he continued, "I'll have to switch to night school after this semester, but I can do that. And we can still have weekends! It's not much pay starting out, but it's enough to maybe get myself a small apartment if I can get my mom's nursing situation buckled in. I'm sure I can. Her nurse now is great, and I could find something close by, in case I needed to get over here."

"Wow, that's amazing! I'm so happy for you," Carissa exclaimed. This was awesome.

"So what was your news?" he asked.

"Well, I mean, after all that, I'm not sure my news even qualifies as news. I'm so proud of you!"

"I think your news is still news. Anything that you're excited about, I'm excited about. Spill it!" he ordered, and she could hear him grinning.

She told him, and he acted like she had said she had a full-time job and was moving into her own place, too. Her news wasn't nearly as big, but you wouldn't have known it from his reaction.

"You get so excited over everything I do," she told him.

"Love does that. You excite me," he laughed. "I can't help it. I love you!"

The tone of his voice made her smile. "I do have that effect on you."

"Yes, you do," he agreed.

They hung up, and Carissa did her nighttime routine and crawled into bed. She would check her email again tomorrow and respond to the ones she hadn't gotten to. Today had been a big day, and she was exhausted. It was time for sleep.

* * *

It had been a week since Connie first emailed about the support group chapters being all in. Since then, Carissa had been swamped with email after email of families sharing their diagnosis and prognosis stories, all of them the same. Doctors filled parents' heads with falsehood after falsehood, tragic prediction after tragic prediction, all pointing to very bleak outcomes for babies with spina bifida.

Carissa was worn down and fired up by the stories, all at the same time. She desperately wanted to make a difference for the next generation of babies like her. It just shouldn't be this way.

Parents should be given factual information on which to base these decisions. This was life or death. Their decisions should at least be based in truth.

All Carissa could do for now, though, was continue to wait. Annabelle had yet to return the email asking how to move forward with plans to make a law. Carissa certainly didn't know where to start. Her high school government teacher had been the varsity football coach, and grades were often based on how much football trivia you knew, rather than whether you knew how to get a law passed. Carissa had been doomed on both sides of that equation. She had been lucky to get out of that class alive. She had passed, though, and that was just as scary as the fact that they let the football coach teach government.

Isaac had started his new job, so she was seeing less of him. He spent his mornings in class, his afternoons at the hospital, and most evenings looking for an apartment near enough to his mom that he could pop in as needed.

She had plenty to do, though, with all the emails piling in from the families within the support group, but it was still hard to see him only on weekends. It would be worth it, though, when he had his own place. She was sure that would give him a sense of accomplishment.

The semester was almost over, too, so she figured she might as well get used to not seeing him as much. He'd be going non-stop with the job becoming full time and night classes starting. And, with her starting school again, weekends would really be all they had. They were really getting somewhere in life, though, and she was proud of that.

Someday, it would all be worth the sacrifice of a little time.

CHAPTER 42

Annabelle had been out of work for a week due to her daughter being hospitalized. It always shocked her how fast a kidney infection came on in a kid with spina bifida. One day, everything was fine. The next day, fever, pain, vomiting, and urine you could smell down the street.

Annabelle was so versed in these infections that she could identify the bacteria by the smell before the urinalysis came back from the lab. It had been e. coli, again, and this time her daughter had come down hard. She'd ended up in the hospital on IV antibiotics and fluids. The vomiting and fever didn't stop for four days.

Annabelle was still exhausted from Isabella's long illness, but she had to get back to work to pay the medical bills that were sure to come in soon. Even with insurance, these hospital stays were expensive for a single mother. She felt terrible, but she had left her still-recovering daughter in the care of a babysitter so she could come back to work today.

There were piles of paperwork and tons of emails. Annabelle trudged through it all until she thought her eyeballs might pop out of her head, and then she ran into the email that perked her right back up. Connie had gotten back to her about the law she and Carissa had spoken about, and it was great news. They had a lot of support from within the community, and all they needed was for Annabelle to tell them how to get started.

Well, she could certainly do that. She began to type.

Connie and Carissa,

I am sorry to be so late in returning this email. I was away from work with a sick daughter. Those kidney infections can be such a beast. But enough about me.

Here's what you need to get started. First, you need to find a sponsor in the Legislature. Usually this is your own district representative. There are lawyers there in his office whose only job is to help people like you do things like this. Call the sponsor and tell him about the law you want passed. He'll have a lawyer put it into proper legal language and send you the draft. Make sure that what the lawyer wrote sounds the same as what you want to accomplish. If it does, the lawyer will then present the bill to the House of Representatives.

The Speaker of the House will then hand the bill off to a committee that will decide whether the bill should be brought to the floor for a vote. This is where you start praying. We could get stalled here because, even if the committee decides to bring the bill forward, the Speaker can decide to throw it out, and we'll have to wait two years to bring it forward again. We don't want to wait another two years. These babies have waited long enough to be heard.

We want this done this session. They meet again in January, and it's November now, so we need to get started.

Carissa, this is your baby, so you take off
with it! Let me know if you need help.

– Annabelle Jenkins

Annabelle sent out the email and called Jane, the babysitter, to check on Isabella.

"Hello?" Jane answered quickly, after only two rings.

"Hey, Jane. How's my girl doing?" Annabelle asked, hoping the news was good.

"She seems okay," Jane replied. "She ate some cereal a little bit ago, and she's lying down playing with her toy horses now. Everything looks good here."

Relieved, Annabelle loosened up and slumped into her chair. "Great! Thank you so much for watching her. You know you're the only one I trust when she's sick."

"I know. I've got her. I'll call if we need you."

"Thanks. Tell her I love her and I'll be home soon. Bye." Annabelle hung up the phone and was able to get some work done, knowing that Isabella was in good hands.

CHAPTER 43

Carissa woke up sometime in the middle of the night with nausea and excruciating pain in her head, and she knew. She'd felt this before and she knew what was coming.

Her shunt was malfunctioning. The tube in her brain that kept the spinal fluid from pooling up and swelling in her brain was clogged. Without help, the fluid would become too much and cause brain damage. She could feel it happening, but the pain was so intense she couldn't get out of bed or even call out for her parents. She reached for her phone on the bedside table, but only managed to knock it onto the floor, and then the darkness came. She felt it swallowing her, but she couldn't fight it off.

"Mom…" she managed to choke out, but she knew it wasn't loud enough for anyone to hear, and then darkness overtook her.

* * *

Jim shook Sarah awake. It was Saturday, and he'd agreed to take her on a breakfast date to IHOP, just the two of them. It was Sarah's favorite place to eat. Carissa could make her own breakfast. They were due some kid-free time.

"Honey, wake up!" he called. "I hear waffles calling your name. And you don't even have to cook them!"

"Ugh..." Sarah replied.

"Come on," Jim ordered. "Date time! You can go in your pajamas. I won't tell anyone!"

Sarah rolled out of bed and went into the bathroom. "I can't go on a date in my pajamas. Give me a minute."

"If you insist, but hurry! My stomach needs a waffle in a bad way."

"I'm coming. Should we tell Carissa we're leaving?" Sarah asked.

"Nope! No kids 'til after breakfast," Jim said. "You know how she hates to be bothered in the morning. Leave her alone. She can take care of herself."

"Okay. No kids! I'm gonna get a quick shower."

After Sarah's shower, they left Carissa there alone.

Jim and Sarah excitedly got into the car and sped away. "I've missed you," Jim said, stealing glances at Sarah as he drove.

"I've missed you, too," Sarah responded, meeting eyes with him.

"We've spent so much time helping Carissa recover, I barely remember what it's like to have some time with just you." Jim told her. "It'll be nice to just be us for a minute, won't it?"

"It's always nice to just be us. We don't do it enough." Sarah smiled at him.

CHAPTER 44

Isaac had gotten out of bed extra early on this Saturday. He had been eyeing an apartment complex nearer to school, and today he had an appointment to see if he could qualify to move in. It would make things easier all around if he could get his own apartment, and he was excited to start a new chapter. He pulled into the complex and found the leasing office right on time. It was 8:30 on the dot. He parked in the nearest open spot and went in.

At the front desk, he found a middle-aged woman wearing a bright green business suit with her silver blonde hair in a tight bun.

"Hello, ma'am. I'm Isaac Carter. I spoke to someone earlier this week on the phone. I'm looking to get a one-bedroom here, wheelchair-accessible." Isaac held his hand out.

"Oh, yes, sir." She reached out to meet his handshake. "Let me just grab your file." She sat down and reached into a drawer in her desk. "I'm Mary. I'm the one you spoke to. Have a seat."

Isaac took one of two brown leather chairs across from Mary.

"Ah, here we go. Isaac Carter." She pulled a group of papers out that were stapled together. "Now, you say you need a wheelchair-accessible apartment? Are you the disabled?"

"No, ma'am. Other people will be visiting that need the accessibility."

"So, you yourself are not disabled?" She took out a notepad and wrote something Isaac couldn't see.

"No." He started to wonder if this would be a problem.

"Tell you what. Let me go talk to my supervisor about this. I'm not sure this is normally something we do, handing out the accessible units to able people, but let me run the situation by her and see what she says." Mary got up from the desk, taking Isaac's paperwork and her notepad with her.

After a long wait, and explaining to a hefty Hispanic woman with glasses that he was primary caregiver for his disabled mother, Isaac left the leasing office of his new apartment complex with keys in hand. He was excited to call Carissa to tell her the good news, and almost as excited to start moving. His mom now had a fantastic nurse, and even someone to stay with her overnight for emergencies, since Isaac wouldn't be there anymore.

He got in his car and called Carissa's cell. After four rings, the call went to voicemail. It was unusual that she didn't answer, but it was early on a Saturday morning, and she did love her sleep. He considered stopping by… he was sure she wouldn't mind… but decided to leave a brief voicemail and wait until she called back to spill the news instead.

"Hey, sleepy head! Call me when you wake up. Don't sleep too late. I love you," and he hung up.

He decided to call his mom next. "Ma, guess what?" he practically yelled into the phone when she picked up.

"What, baby?" Betty asked.

"I got that apartment I was looking at," he told her. "I made the first month's rent, and they gave me a key. I can start moving in as soon as I'm ready. They even gave me the accessible unit so you can come by any time you feel like it."

"That's great! Now come get your stuff out of my house, boy. I've been waiting almost nineteen years for this," she joked.

But he knew this was probably the hardest thing she'd been through in her life. Her boy was grown up, getting his own place, and starting a life on his own.

He wouldn't let her down, no matter what.

CHAPTER 45

J im and Sarah sat in a booth, enjoying breakfast at their usual get-away spot. It had been too long, with Carissa's surgery and everything else, since they'd had time for just the two of them.

"I've missed this," Jim said, cutting off a piece of his waffle.

"Me, too," Sarah replied. "Hopefully, Carissa will be out of the woods medically for a while, and we can do more of it. I do enjoy a good private waffle with you."

"Speaking of the kid, what's going on with this law thing she keeps talking about?" Jim asked. "You're around to catch more of it than I am. I can hardly keep up."

"Well, apparently she has a lot of support from the spina bifida community, but she hasn't heard back from the lady who's supposed to tell her how to get everything in motion." Sarah took a long, satisfying drink of her coffee. "She's still waiting. I think it's been a week or more. I hope this woman didn't just drop her. She'll be so disappointed."

"Wow, I hope she hears back soon, with school starting back," Jim said, a touch of worry in his voice. "I don't see how she'll have time to be so involved with it and still go back to school, and she IS going back to school."

"Yeah, between this and school and Isaac, I don't know how she'll keep her head above water if she doesn't get this stuff out of the way soon." Sarah echoed Jim's anxious look.

They finished up breakfast and debated taking a ride down to Galveston to the beach.

"Carissa said she and Isaac went the other night, and he carried her down to the water," Sarah said. "Seems like they're getting pretty serious."

"Hopefully not too serious," he said, only half-joking. "I heard he's getting his own place soon. I hope they don't get themselves into too much trouble with no adult supervision."

"Yeah, let's hope not. We've taught her, but who knows what'll happen when temptation comes. Speaking of that, I'm sure Isaac is chomping at the bit to come over. Let's skip the beach and beat him there," Sarah said.

They went back to the car and started toward home. When they got there, Carissa still wasn't awake. There was no sign of coffee or any other breakfast making.

"Good grief, Jim," Sarah exclaimed. "She's still in bed. Teenagers! This is ridiculous. I'm going to wake her up. She can't just lay in bed all day. I don't care if it is Saturday," Sarah headed toward Carissa's room to wake her.

Jim plopped in front of the television to let his waffle settle. Currently, it was piercing what he was sure was a lung.

"Jim, call 911!" he heard Sarah scream from the other room. "She won't wake up!"

Jim jumped off the couch and ran into Carissa's bedroom,

where he found his wife hovering over his unconscious daughter. He felt his knees go weak. All this time they'd been gone. How long had she been like this?

"Is she breathing?" he choked out.

"Yes, but it's shallow! Call 911!"

Jim fumbled his phone out of his pocket. He was shaking so hard he could barely dial the number.

"Yes, my daughter is in bed unconscious! I don't know how long! She has spina bifida and hydrocephalus! Please hurry! Yes, she's breathing! I don't know! Just come!" he shouted into the phone.

The ambulance seemed to take forever. Carissa couldn't be roused, no matter what Jim or Sarah did. They tried shaking her, screaming, pouring cold water on her, and she just laid there through all of it.

"Oh, please, God, we can't lose her!" Sarah cried out.

There was a knock at the front door. Jim ran to get it. It was the paramedics. He let them in and led them to Carissa's bedroom. It was like something out of a movie. Jim was sure he left his body as he watched these men put lines into Carissa's body and an oxygen mask over her face. They transferred her to the ambulance gurney and had her in the back of the ambulance in less than three minutes. Jim and Sarah both climbed in after her.

"We can only take one of you," one of the paramedics said.

"We're both going in this ambulance," Jim countered with more authority than he knew he had in him.

The paramedic didn't argue. He just shut the door, and the driver turned the siren on. The ambulance shrieked all the way to the hospital while Jim and Sarah gave the best medical history they could.

"She's got spina bifida and hydrocephalus. She just had tethered cord surgery about two months ago," Jim yelled over the sound of the siren.

"Has she been complaining of anything recently? Pain? Any illness that you know of?" the paramedic asked.

"No. Nothing. No complaints, but she's a pretty tough kid. She doesn't complain much," Sarah responded.

They pulled into the emergency room entrance, and the paramedic shoved the doors of the ambulance open. He lowered the gurney carrying Carissa onto the concrete, and began pushing her into the hospital. Jim and Sarah hurried behind him.

"Patient's name is Carissa Schultz. Unconscious eighteen-year-old female, history of spina bifida, tethered cord, and hydrocephalus. Vital signs are normal except for slight bradycardia and altered state of awareness. These are her parents. They say she has had no complaints recently."

"You're the parents?" the emergency room doctor asked Jim and Sarah.

"Yes," they answered in unison.

"How long has she been like this?" he asked.

"We don't know. We found her in her bedroom after we got home from going out to breakfast this morning," Sarah answered.

The doctor looked at her searchingly. "And she was fine this morning before you left for breakfast?"

Sarah shook her head guiltily. She hadn't checked on Carissa.

"We don't know, doctor. We're not sure when this started. She was fine when she went to bed last night," Jim replied, now holding onto Sarah.

"Okay, we'll run some tests. Have a seat in the waiting room and we'll come get you when we find something."

Jim and Sarah did as they were told, going out to the emergency waiting room.

Sarah clutched his hand. "Jim, what's wrong with her? Why didn't we check on her? We should have checked on her!"

"I don't know," he said, patting her hands to calm her. "I don't know what's wrong. The doctors will find it."

"My poor baby. How long was she alone like that? How long, Jim?"

"Sarah, I don't know. She was never alone because God was with her. We have to trust Him." It was all Jim could think to say. He felt just as guilty for not checking on her as Sarah did. Why hadn't they? It would have taken just a second.

"We should call Isaac. Carissa would want him here," Sarah said through tears.

"Okay, I'll do it. You stay right here, and I'll call him from outside. Come get me if you hear anything."

Jim stepped outside to make the phone call to Isaac. Between rings, he tried to stifle the lump catching in his throat.

"Hello?" Isaac answered.

Jim took a breath. "Isaac."

"Oh, hey, Mr. Schultz, what's up?"

"Look, we, uh… Carissa… Isaac, you need to come to the hospital. Carissa is really sick. We're not sure what's going on yet. She'd want you here, though. Come on up."

"What? What do you mean, really sick? Is she okay? I'm coming," Isaac replied, worry filling his voice.

"I really don't know, Isaac. We just found her… look, just come on up. We'll talk when you get here." Jim ended the call. He couldn't bear to talk anymore, and he didn't want to tell Isaac how serious it was over the phone.

CHAPTER 46

Isaac heard the line go dead. Panic set in. What was wrong with Carissa?

He couldn't even think. He got in his car and headed straight to the hospital, praying the whole way. He had called Carissa this morning. Why hadn't she answered? Was she that sick?

On the way to the hospital, every stop light seemed to take forever. He needed to get there. What was going on? What had Mr. Schultz not wanted to say?

He was hiding something, Isaac was sure. How bad was this? "God, please help her!" he cried out, speeding as fast as he thought he could get away with.

When he arrived, he saw Mr. and Mrs. Schultz in a corner of the waiting room, sitting down and holding onto one another.

"What's going on?" he called out, making his way toward them.

"We found Carissa this morning, very sick. She was unconscious, and we couldn't wake her up. The doctors are running tests, but we still don't know anything. We're just waiting," Jim told him.

"Unconscious? I just talked to her last night! She was fine." Isaac felt like he'd been hit by a semi.

"People with spina bifida have a lot of underlying conditions, Isaac," Jim said in a strained tone. "Things can hit out of nowhere and go downhill fast. It could be any number of things that did this so quickly."

Sarah nodded. "We just have to trust God and the doctors."

Isaac turned around in his seat and put his head in his hands. He couldn't believe it. She was fine yesterday, and now no one knew what was wrong, only that it was bad enough that she was unconscious. He wanted to tell her about his new apartment. He wanted to hear about progress with her law. He wanted things to be normal. He just wanted Carissa back.

They sat for a long time, hearing nothing, and then a nurse came out to talk to them. "Are you all with Ms. Schultz?"

"Yes, I'm her mother," Sarah replied.

"Okay. Here's what we've got." The nurse was noncommittal, professional. "It looks like Carissa has a few things going on. First, she has a bladder infection, common with spina bifida. I'm sure you know that. We've started treatment for it, but that's not the big issue here. The big issue seems to be that Carissa's shunt failed. There's a clog or a break somewhere in the tubing, and we need to repair it. She'll need surgery right away." She looked at Carissa's parents. "We need your consent to operate."

"Absolutely. Where do I sign?" Sarah said, sounding like her breath had been sucked right out of her.

The nurse took Sarah to a desk just inside the emergency room doors to fill out the paperwork. Jim and Isaac stayed behind.

"What does all this mean?" Isaac asked, scared to hear the answer.

"She needs brain surgery. There's a tube going from her brain into her abdominal cavity, called a shunt, that draws spinal fluid off her brain," Jim explained. "A normal brain does this on its own. Carissa's never did, so when she was a baby, they put the shunt in to prevent brain damage. The shunt is clogged. She needs a new one. Things should be fine once she gets the new one, but it is brain surgery."

"Brain surgery… but she'll be okay?"

"She should be." Jim didn't sound very sure.

Sarah walked back out into the waiting room and sat down. "All set," she said.

"Did you see her?" Isaac asked.

"No. They're already prepping for surgery. They say the fluid build-up is pretty bad. She needs to get it taken care of right now."

Isaac hung his head down. He wasn't sure he was strong enough for this. In fact, he was sure he wasn't. He loved her so much, but he hated everything about spina bifida.

They waited in the emergency waiting room. Jim offered a few times to buy drinks or snacks for everyone, but no one could eat. Isaac paced the room until he got dizzy. Sarah sat in her chair with her arms wrapped around her chest, kind of hugging herself for comfort.

After about two hours, a man came out, dressed in familiar surgeon garb. He approached them and sat down to talk.

"Carissa did well. She's not awake yet, so it's hard to tell if there will be any permanent damage from this. The fluid build-up was bad, and it's hard to tell how long she was like that. We'll know more in the next few hours as the anesthesia wears off. They're getting her into a room on the third floor now, and I'll let you know when you can go up and see her. Do you have any questions for me?"

"No. Thank you, doctor," Jim replied.

Eventually, they were cleared to go up to the third floor to see Carissa. They were silent, lost in their own thoughts, on the way up. Sarah still wouldn't let go of her chest. Isaac mostly looked at the floor in the elevator, and Jim tried to think of ways to comfort his family. This was hard. He wasn't sure anything he said would be helpful, so he stayed quiet.

They arrived in the room to find Carissa still sleeping. She looked comfortable at least, but Isaac thought she should be waking up more by now. He stood by her bedside and looked at all the bandages and wires, and he began to tear up. Seeing her like this broke his heart. He had seen his mother in the hospital, but he was little the last time she had had surgery. He didn't remember it. Now he was scared for Carissa on a level he hadn't experienced before. This was hard. He would have given anything in that moment for her to open her eyes and tell him about her law, or tell him about anything. He gently stroked the hand that didn't have an IV coming out of it, and she stirred a little and opened her eyes, just a crack.

"We have to stop meeting like this," she mumbled, and grasped his hand.

Isaac couldn't hold back anymore. Tears filled his eyes and streamed down his face. "I love you so much. Please don't ever scare me like that again."

"I promise, but only if you get me a Dr. Pepper."

"I'm right on top of that," Isaac replied, as he wiped the tears from his face. He left in search of her soda.

He decided to call his mom. "Yeah, Mom. They said it was a shunt malfunction. I don't really know, but it was bad. She looks good now, though. I think she's okay. She asked for Dr. Pepper. In fact, I'm back at the room now. I'll call you back when I know more. Love you."

Isaac entered the room with a Dr. Pepper in his hand. "Hey, guys, any more news?"

"Not much. She's sleeping again. The doctor hasn't been in yet," Jim replied.

"Man, that was so bad! Does this happen to her often? I mean, have you guys ever seen anything like that?" Isaac asked.

"Not like that. She's had malfunctions before, but the last one came on slowly. We had a few days' warning, and we were able to get her into surgery before anything like this happened. This just came out of nowhere," Sarah told him.

Isaac set the Dr. Pepper on the small table beside Carissa's bed and stared at her. Was he ready for this to be his reality? His girlfriend could collapse at any moment? Her parents said this wasn't common and had never happened this bad to her before, but what if it did? Could he handle it? She had really scared him.

"Hey, folks! How's my patient doing?" the doctor from the emergency room came around the corner with a clipboard and pen in his hands.

"She seems to be okay. She talked to us some, and then went back to sleep," Jim answered.

"How did she seem cognitively? Does she seem to be herself? Any deficits? It's early, but did you notice anything?"

"She seems fine," Jim told him. "She asked for a Dr. Pepper. That's usually our cue that whatever ails her is on its way out."

"Good. I'll approve the Dr. Pepper, as long as she takes it slow and it stays down. We'll see if we can get her a light dinner later on. If that stays down and she feels okay, we'll evaluate for cognitive issues in the morning and send her home with orders to follow up with her regular neurosurgeon if everything looks okay."

"Sounds good, Doctor. Thank you," Jim replied.

The doctor left the room, and Carissa popped her eyes open. "Is he gone?" she asked, sounding a little more alert than before.

"Yeah, did you need him?" Isaac asked.

"No. I just didn't want him to know I was awake. I hate doctors."

Jim, Sarah and Isaac all laughed at that. Carissa was back. They were sure now.

Sarah pushed the button to raise Carissa's bed a bit so she could drink her Dr. Pepper. "Let me know if you get a headache, and I'll lower it back down some."

Carissa smiled weakly. "I'm okay. Nothing compares to the headache I had yesterday. I knew what was happening, and I tried to call out, but I couldn't. What happened? How did you guys find me? Did I pass out?"

"Yes. We found you unconscious in bed this morning. You were breathing, but you wouldn't wake up. Dad even poured water on your head. Have you been having headaches?" Sarah replied.

"Yeah, I mean, just small ones. I didn't think anything of it."

"Carissa, you can't let things like that go! You know that." Sarah was alarmed.

"I know now…" Carissa replied.

Carissa finished her Dr. Pepper without getting sick, and they all passed hospital time by playing a mean game of spades with some cards someone had left in the room in a drawer. They were glad for the find, but none of them was sure what it said for the cleaning staff at the hospital. Boredom had set in so hard, though, that they didn't care.

Once again, the Schultz girls took the game day title, and the boys were left to sulk.

"Carissa beat us, even after brain surgery," Isaac joked. "What does that even say? Should we throw in the towel?"

"Never!" Jim declared. "A man never throws in the towel, even when he's losing. Especially in the case of brain surgery!"

"Whatever you say, Mr. Schultz," Isaac laughed. "Whatever you say."

Carissa's dinner arrived, and once everyone was sure she would keep it down, the rest of the family went down to the café on the first floor to scrounge up whatever dinner they could find.

"Good luck out there, guys!" Carissa called jokingly as they made their way out of the room in search of something that resembled food.

* * *

When she was finally alone, the reality of the day hit her. She had been ignoring her headaches for a while. She hadn't told anyone because she didn't want it to get in the way of her life. She was so tired of spina bifida interrupting everything. She had just wanted it, for once, to take a back seat.

It certainly hadn't gone that way. She'd almost been stubborn enough to lose her life. She had been so dumb. It scared her, and she promised in that moment to take better care of herself, no matter what it took. The look on her parents' and Isaac's faces had told her how serious this was, and she never wanted be responsible for putting those looks on their faces again.

CHAPTER 47

The cognitive testing went well the next day, and Carissa was released to go home. Isaac hung around the house for a bit, just to make sure she was okay. They watched television and played board games from the couch.

"Do you want some ice cream?" Isaac asked her. "My mom brought me ice cream when I had my tonsils out. It made me feel better."

"That's because your throat hurt, you goof!" Carissa replied.

"Hey, ice cream is medicine in any circumstance. Take it or leave it, woman."

"Take it," she declared, and Isaac popped up and headed toward the kitchen.

He returned minutes later with an ice cream sandwich in each hand. "One for the patient, one for the doctor," he announced.

"Fair enough," Carissa answered, reaching for one of the sandwiches. She unwrapped it and took the biggest bite she could manage which, of course, resulted in brain freeze. "Oww… Too fast! Too fast!" she cried out.

"Are you okay?" Isaac asked, turning toward her, trying to judge the severity of what was happening.

"Brain freeze is the opposite of fun right after brain surgery. I'm fine. Owww…" Carissa assured him.

Isaac relaxed back into the couch, and put his arm around her. This scare had sure done a number on his nerves. He wondered if he'd ever be able to relax again after seeing her go through everything she had gone through. He loved her, though, more than anything in the world. If this experience had taught him nothing else, it had taught him that.

"You really scared me, you know. I don't know what I would have done if things had gotten any worse. This whole thing made me realize how much you mean to me. I don't ever want to lose you, or see you go through anything like that again. Please take care of yourself," he told her, tears welling up in his eyes.

Carissa snuggled up against him. "I know, Isaac. I scared me, too. I guess I just wanted something in my life to be a 'normal' headache." She gazed up at him. "I'm sorry. I'll be more careful. I love you too much to scare you like that again."

"I love you, too," he replied, and they sat silently on the couch for a while, finishing their ice cream sandwiches.

It wasn't long before Carissa was asleep in the crook of Isaac's arm, and he wouldn't have had her anywhere else. He let her sleep like that for a long time, his arm going numb, until it was time for him to go home. He hated to wake her, but his mom would be worried, and he had to pack for moving into his new apartment.

"Baby," he called out quietly, wiggling his arm out from under her. "Babe."

"Hmmm…" she mumbled. "Oh, I fell asleep. I'm so sorry."

She swept hair out of her face and sat up.

"It's okay. It was nice having you there in my arms. I need to go, though. It's late." He helped her sweep the rest of the hair out of her face, and his hand gently stroked her cheek. "I love you. I'll text you when I get home."

"I love you, too," she replied, still sleepy. He kissed her good-bye, and left her on the couch.

CHAPTER 48

C arissa woke up sometime in the darkest part of the night, and it took her a minute to realize she was still on the couch where Isaac had left her.

"Ugh…" she mumbled to herself, and flopped over into her wheelchair to make her way to her bedroom. On the way there, she remembered everything going on with Connie Peterson and Annabelle Jenkins. Where had they left off? She couldn't remember. She had been so foggy up until her shunt malfunction.

When she got to her room, she decided she couldn't wait until morning to get back in the game. She booted up the laptop, and found just the email she was looking for. On the same day she had gotten sick, Annabelle had sent an email addressed to both Carissa and Connie, outlining the steps needed to get the law passed.

Carissa's heart jumped into her throat. Could she contact her local representative in the middle of the night? Did that look crazy? Did she care? If she came off less than sane, she could certainly blame brain surgery, she thought. But who was her representative? College Algebra had failed her here. It had done nothing toward teaching her how to navigate the real world. She didn't need to know how X's relationship was with Y. She didn't care. That was their business. She needed to know how to save these babies!

She didn't know who her representative was, but she knew who would know. Google knew everything, and it didn't take Carissa long to find the information she needed, including a valid email address and phone number. Obviously, calling at whatever-dark-thirty was not an option, so she opted for email.

It didn't take her long to figure out what she wanted to say, and her fingers flew across the keys. All she needed was one chance to tell her story, one opportunity to get in front of this John Walker and tell him how things needed to change, and why. This email was her one chance to get there.

Dear Mr. Walker,

My name is Carissa Schultz. I am an 18-year-old woman born with spina bifida, and I need your help. I, along with several others in the spina bifida community, am interested in getting a law passed that would force Obstetrics and Gynecology physicians to fully educate themselves about the diagnosis and prognosis of spina bifida before handing out the diagnosis and offering abortion to expecting or new parents. In my experience, doctors are not well enough educated to truthfully handle a new diagnosis of spina bifida. They are educated only to the point of the technology available at the time they went to medical school, and some medical schools are even using outdated textbooks.

This issue is leading to the needless abortion of possibly

thousands of perfectly viable pregnancies, and the deaths of many valuable, contributing members of our world. Please help those of us in the spina bifida community give the next generation the best possible chance at life by assisting us in making this law. We do not ask for a ban on abortion. This is not even a pro-life or pro-choice issue. It is a truth issue. These parents deserve all the truthful information they can receive to make an informed decision about the future of their families. Thank you for your time and attention to this matter. I await your response.

– Carissa Schultz

There. It was done. Everything she had set out to do was now in motion and out of her hands. All that was left to do was wait on a response, and she was sure she wouldn't get one at this hour. She decided to shut things down and go to sleep. She would email Annabelle and Connie in the morning to let them know the ball was rolling.

She crawled into bed, asked God to put His hand into her work, and found sleep quickly and peacefully.

CHAPTER 49

Annabelle Jenkins arrived at her office early on Monday morning, hoping to catch up on all the paperwork she had missed when her daughter was in the hospital. There were still mountains of it, and she wasn't sure she'd ever get to the bottom of it.

She sat down at her desk with her coffee, yawned, and booted up her computer for the day. Upon opening her email, she found a pleasant surprise.

Dear Annabelle and Connie,

I am very sorry to be so late in getting back with you both about the law. I had a very serious shunt malfunction and ended up needing surgery. I'm now well on my way to recovery, though, and have emailed my local representative, Mr. John Walker, letting him know our intentions. I guess all we can do now is wait until I hear back from him, but I wanted to let you both know we're making progress. I look forward to continuing to work with both of you on this.

– Carissa

Annabelle closed out the email and immediately called Connie. Paperwork could wait.

Connie answered, more quickly than Annabelle anticipated.

"Connie, it's Annabelle. Have you checked your email?"

"No. I haven't even sat down at my desk yet," Connie said. "My phone rang before I even put my purse down. Why? What's going on?"

"You need to tell everyone in your groups that we're well on the way to getting this law passed… the one where doctors have to tell us the truth about spina bifida. Gather the troops. This is happening," Annabelle said, new energy in her voice.

"Wow, really?" Connie replied. "I had all but given up on it. We hadn't heard back from Carissa in so long, I thought she'd abandoned us."

"She was sick. Shunt malfunction. Figures."

Connie nodded, even though she knew Annabelle couldn't see her. "Yeah. Spina bifida rears its ugly head… literally… again. But she's okay, though?"

"She says she's good. She's emailing the big dogs. I think it's time to get excited!" Annabelle exclaimed.

"I'll send an email out to all my leaders today and let them know. I'm sure they'll be all over this. You wouldn't believe the stories I've heard that directly match exactly what Carissa is trying to put a stop to."

"I think I would believe them," Annabelle replied.

They ended the conversation and Connie got to work, emailing as fast as her fingers would go.

Dear Leaders,

Sometime back, as you will recall, I told you all about a young woman with spina bifida who was working hard to bring forth a law that would require doctors to tell the truth about spina bifida diagnosis and prognosis. I'm happy to announce that, after some rough patches with her own health, she is now well on her way to making this dream a reality. Please let your group members know, and let's get behind her and let our government know we're with her all the way. Contact your local representatives. Let them know we all want this.

– Connie Peterson

Within hours, leaders began returning the email. The excitement was palpable. Everyone was behind Carissa and her cause. No one wanted these babies to die without reason. No one wanted new parents to be given false information any longer, whether intentional or not.

People committed to calling their representatives every day. People offered to go to the capitol in January to speak out for the bill. Some people were even planning to take their children to the capitol so they could speak for themselves about how this bill would have helped settle their own parents' anxiety.

Everyone wanted a hand in it. Everyone was ready to help. Connie was overwhelmed with emails that first day, and it didn't let up for weeks. This was going to be huge, and it deserved to be. Countless babies had already died needlessly. There didn't need to be one more.

Come January, a mighty army was going to make sure these tragedies stopped.

CHAPTER 50

I saac moved the last of his boxes into his new apartment, and slowly but surely unpacked each one. He was a man on his own now, with a good job, school well underway, and Carissa.

He sat on the couch he was renting to own from the local furniture store, and thought about the future. He was going to be a doctor one day. He'd be able to support himself well. It wouldn't always be rental furniture and his old beat-up Volvo. One day soon, he'd be providing a good life for himself. He hoped to make enough to give his mother a little something, and he knew for sure the future he dreamed of wasn't the same if Carissa wasn't part of it. He hadn't seen her in days, and he missed her like crazy. Isaac couldn't imagine not having her in his life. She was his everything. They had been dating only a few months, but man, that girl got him all stupid when he thought of her. It was late, but he had to text her.

"Hey, babe, what's going on?" he sent.

She didn't take long to respond. "Hey, you, how's the new place? Loving that independence yet?"

"It's good! Missing you, though. All this work and school is making me nuts, not being able to see you."

"I miss you, too. It'll all be worth it soon enough, though, Dr. Carter."

"That has a good ring to it, you know. Dr. Carter," he replied.

"It really does," Carissa texted back.

They ended the conversation with text love and kisses, and Isaac dreamed of the day he wouldn't have to say goodbye to her anymore.

He made one more phone call before he went to bed.

"Ma, everything okay? Do you need anything? Your nurse is there?"

"I'm fine, Isaac," Betty said. "Just got in from celebrating with the girls that your stinky butt is out of my house!" She laughed, and he enjoyed the sound, missing being home for a moment.

"Okay, Ma, if you say so. I'll leave my phone by my bed all night. Call me if you need anything, and I'll be right there. The nurse has my number, too. Tell her not to hesitate to call. I love you!"

"I love you, too, son, and I'll call if I need anything. Right now, all I need is sleep, and you do, too! And hey, I'm the mother. You call if you need anything, boy," Betty told him.

"All right, you're the mom," he agreed. "I'll call you if I need anything."

"Good boy. Tell Carissa I said 'hello.' I know she's over there."

"She's actually not, Ma," Isaac said. "I've decided we'll see each other at her parents' house for now. I don't want to bring her over here. Things might get… well, you know. You raised me better than that. I respect her. Not until we're married."

"Isaac, I'm so proud of the man you've become," Betty told him, pride ringing in her voice, "and I have to say, that can't all be my raisin'. Most of that is God's hand. I can't take credit."

"Well, you and God did a good enough job that I know better than to take from that girl what isn't mine yet and, if that means we stay at her parents' house, then that's what we'll do. I love you, Ma. Goodnight."

With that, Isaac was alone with his thoughts again. There wasn't much left to do, except end the day in the bed he had brought with him from his mother's house.

CHAPTER 51

It had been a whole month since John Walker had been in this cold office. He had taken some time off to be with his wife after the birth of their baby boy, and it was hard to come back. He'd been gone since November, and there were piles and more piles of paperwork and new emails to get through. He wondered if anyone had even been over to his desk to prevent this paper mountain he was staring at.

Unlikely. No one around here did their own jobs, much less tried to help with the slack when someone was missing. The legislative session started again in January, and it might take him that long to sift through this mess.

With a sigh and a cup of coffee, he faced the stack and got to work.

It ended up taking him until his lunch break just to organize it into stacks he could deal with. He ripped open the lunch his wife packed and ate a turkey sandwich while he checked his emails.

"Good grief..." he sighed, looking at the extensive list. There were hundreds. It was nearly impossible to organize them by priority, but he did. He organized them into things he had to get to today, things he had to get to before the next legislative session, and things that could wait until he could see above the papers on his desk. Just the "today" emails would take him until sometime next week, he thought, but he settled into his chair and started at the beginning. Some of the things in his "today" stack consisted of things that only required "yes" or "no" answers, and honestly would have only required a little help from Google if people had bothered. At least those would be out of the way quickly.

About halfway through the pile, when his head was spinning, he ran across one from a woman named Carissa. It was clearly misfiled, and belonged in the "before the next legislative session" pile, but the subject line caught his eye. "Spina Bifida Law: Tell the Truth."

Spina bifida. They had tested his son for that, hadn't they? Told his wife that, if he had it, he would be mentally retarded, that he'd never walk or talk, or even go to the bathroom on his own. He was sure they had tested for it. They didn't find anything but, man, the wait was scary.

Yes. This was the thing they had been testing for. He remembered, and he was curious enough to open this email now to see what this woman wanted with spina bifida. Surely she didn't have it, or she wouldn't be emailing him. She'd be a vegetable. And she couldn't have a kid with it. Didn't most of those babies get aborted?

That's what the doctor had said, that if their boy had this, they could just abort and try again. Luckily, they didn't have to deal with that. Their boy was happy and healthy, just the way he was supposed to be.

He skimmed through the email quickly, then went back to read it a second time, just to make sure he'd read it right. Pausing, resting his chin on his hands, he wasn't sure what to think.

Okay, so this woman claimed to actually have spina bifida, that wretched birth defect that the doctor had been so negative about. Right. And now she was typing him an email asking him to tell people it wasn't as bad as that doctor said it was?

How was he supposed to believe that? The doctor had been pretty plain. If their son had this, his life wouldn't be worth living. If he even survived at all, he would be a vegetable. The only humane thing to do would be to abort. And here was this woman claiming she had spina bifida?

No way. This had to be some kind of sick joke. "I'm not falling for that," he said to himself, and closed out the email. This girl could find some other fool. He had work to do. John plowed through more emails and, by the end of the day, he was about a quarter done with the "today" emails. But it was time to shut it down and go home to that wife and new baby of his.

"Tony, I'm out." he said to the co-worker in the cubicle next to his.

"Later, John, good to have you back!" Tony replied.

When he got home, he found both his wife and baby asleep on the couch, baby formula spilled on the floor, and a rattle between his wife's toes.

"Must've been a rough one," he thought as he reached down and picked his boy up off his wife's chest. Somehow, between the time he'd left for work and the time he'd gotten home, the baby had traded in his sweet smell for a smell that was much less pleasant. "Let's get you changed, boy! You stink!"

John laid his son on a blanket on the floor and began the terrible process that was diaper changing. He didn't know how his wife did this all day long. He could barely get through one diaper without gagging.

"Burble, burble, gah!" his son cried out, with a half-grin that he hadn't quite mastered yet.

"I hear you talking. Don't wake Mommy up. You wore her out," he whispered back. Looking into his son's eyes, it hit him. What if what this Carissa woman said was true? What if spina bifida wasn't as bad as that doctor had made it sound? He and his wife had been terrified at the thought of their son turning out like that, but what if none of it was true?

What if Carissa really did have spina bifida? She seemed fine. She was obviously capable of sending an email and standing up for herself. What else were these people capable of? And what did it matter?

Looking into his son's eyes, he realized it didn't matter if his son never walked or talked, or did anything beyond what he was doing right now. He was still his son, and he deserved a fair chance to do everything he could do, no matter what that was. And, if what the doctor told him wasn't even true, what better reason to help these other kids out?

"Hey, Tony," he said softly into his cell phone as he put the baby in his crib. "Are you still at the office? Great. Look, I need you to get on my computer. There's an email there. I don't think I deleted it. Carissa Schultz. I need that email, and I need you to see if she left a phone number or anything. If not, find me a phone number. I need to speak to her today. It's important."

John Walker got off the phone armed with Carissa's information, and went in the other room to make the call.

CHAPTER 52

It was Christmas Eve, and Carissa had so much to thank God for. She had been talking back and forth with Annabelle, Connie, and John Walker for some time, and it really looked as if things might go well in the next legislative session.

Things were great with Isaac, even though they weren't seeing much of each other lately with his school and work. It would be worth it, though, when he was a doctor. They just had to keep telling themselves it would all be worth it.

Mom and Dad were good. Dad's job was going well, and Mom was happy as long as her family was happy. Carissa didn't understand how she could be so happy as a housewife, but she was.

Carissa wanted a career. She wanted to be out in all the mess of the world, but Mom was content to change the world right from her own home, and that was good, too. It had certainly worked out for Carissa to have her there.

Things were just really good, and going to church tonight with

Isaac and Betty was the perfect way to thank God for it all. She took one last look in the mirror to make sure her dark blue sweater dress and her makeup were perfect.

She heard Isaac pull up into the driveway and went out to meet him. She climbed into the passenger seat as Isaac put her chair in the back.

"Merry Christmas!" he told her.

"Merry Christmas. Where's your mom?" she asked.

He raised his voice so she could hear him as he closed the trunk. "She'll meet us there. She was out and about with friends when I called, so I couldn't pick her up. She said the girls are coming with her."

Carissa smiled. "Oh, okay. Lady on the town."

"Yeah, that's Ma for ya."

Isaac got in the car and they headed toward the church. When they got there, they found Betty sitting outside waiting for them, alone.

"Hey, Ma, where's the girls?" Isaac asked.

Betty blushed. "Well, Isaac, there's something I wasn't really honest with you about." Just then, a man, larger in build than Isaac, but not taller, walked around the corner. She put a hand on his arm. "This is Eric. We've been seeing each other for a little while now. I hope it's okay that he brought me. The girls, obviously, are not coming. In fact, I may have told a white lie here and there about seeing the girls. I'm sorry. I just wasn't ready for you to meet him."

Isaac eyed the other man for a moment, then nodded. "It's cool, Ma. As long as he treats you well. Hello... Eric... Is there a last name I can call you by, sir?"

"Eric is fine, young man. I'm not that formal," Eric replied.

They shook hands, and Isaac said, "Well, Eric, treat my mama well, and we're all good. Let's go to church."

They all went in and took their seats, Betty in the aisle, Eric beside her. Isaac made sure to sit by him, just to make a presence, and Carissa sat on the other side of Isaac.

The service was enjoyable, and Carissa couldn't help but count her blessings, Isaac and Betty being two of them. It looked as if Eric might squeeze his way in there, too, eventually.

CHAPTER 53

Annabelle, Connie, John and Carissa all met for coffee. It was early January, and the legislative session would be starting soon. They had to get their ducks in a row. John wanted to go over the bill with them and make sure it was everything they wanted it to be.

Annabelle, Connie, and Carissa wanted to make sure they were doing everything they possibly could to make this thing pass.

"Okay, so here's what we have," John said. "Look it over and make sure it's right. If I've left anything important out, now's the time to tell me." He started passing papers around to each of the ladies. "I'll want to change it before I present it. And you guys want to be there on the day we vote, right? I would think the three of you wouldn't have it any other way." When he was done passing out papers, he picked up his coffee cup to warm his hands.

"Right," they answered, almost in unison.

They all looked over the bill as it was written, and everything looked good. Doctors would be required to find the most up-to-date information on spina bifida before handing out a diagnosis. They would be required to research treatment options, to let parents know that there were medical advancements that could help. They would be required to tell the whole truth to new and expecting parents before offering any "options." And parents would be given hope, for once, that their babies with spina bifida could not only survive, but thrive, through their challenges.

"I like it," Carissa said, after taking a sip of her latte. "When do we do this thing?"

"We meet on the second Tuesday in January, which is actually this coming Tuesday. Can you all make it?"

"Absolutely," Connie said. The others agreed and, after some chit-chat, the meeting broke up and they all went their separate ways.

Carissa was an overflowing pot of nerves and excitement. She assumed the coffee wasn't helping calm her any. On her way home, she called Sarah.

"Mom, I have to go to Austin this Tuesday," she said. "It's happening!"

"That's great, hon. So you met with John? How did that go?" Sarah asked. "Well, I assume, considering you're planning a road trip."

"The bill is perfect, Mom. I think we've really got something."

"Awesome, sweetie. I'm so proud of you." Sarah paused, then said, "Let me go tell your dad."

Carissa waited while Sarah went to find Jim, but she came back to the phone without him. "I'll tell him later," she told Carissa. "He's on a business call again, I guess. Those guys never give him a break. But we're so proud of you. You really are a world changer."

"I love you, Mom."

"I love you, too, baby."

Carissa pressed END and then called Isaac, but he didn't answer. He must have been on the other line, so she left a message for him to call back.

CHAPTER 54

"Hey, hon, Carissa called and had news, but you were on the phone," Sarah told Jim as he walked into the kitchen to help her with the dishes. "She's going to Austin this Tuesday for her bill. They're going to try to get it passed this session. Isn't that great? I think we should go with her. I'll wait on the steps. I just want to be with her when she hears, don't you?" Sarah practically bombarded Jim when he was off the phone.

Jim held up his hands with a smile. "Slow down, woman. I think we should go. We need to be there, for a lot of reasons. We'll go, for sure." He wrapped one arm around her and rinsed off a plate with the other hand.

Sarah grinned at him happily. "Good, we should be there. Who was on the phone? Work again? They drive me crazy. Can't you ever just be home?"

"It wasn't work. It was Isaac, actually." Jim grin widened. "He had a question about something."

Sarah perked up. "Is everything okay? What did he need?" She took the plate from his hand, dried it, and put it in the cabinet above her head.

"Just man things. Everything is fine," Jim said. "We worked it out. He's a fine young man, and I'm glad Carissa picked him. I think you are, too."

"Yes, I'm proud of both of them." She looked up at him and smiled, then her face turned more serious. "Do you think this bill will pass? What if it doesn't? What'll that do to Carissa?"

Jim looked down toward her, grabbing another plate to rinse as he did. "I sure hope it does. Surely, people can see the value of just telling the truth. It's not even like she's asking to outlaw abortion entirely. She's just asking for the truth to be told and for parents to be able to make a more educated decision. That certainly can't be looked upon poorly."

"I sure hope you're right. If she's done all this and it doesn't pass, well, I don't even want to think how heartbroken she'll be." Sarah put a cup into the pantry.

"Let's hope we don't even have to think that way. I just have a feeling we'll have some things to celebrate." He drained the water from the sink as he handed Sarah one last fork to put away.

"I hope you're right," Sarah said, taking the fork and putting it in the drawer to her right. She dried out the sink and grabbed a bottle of water from the refrigerator. "You want one?" she asked Jim, handing out the bottle. He took it from her, and she pulled out another for herself, opened it, and took a big gulp.

"I'm right. When am I wrong?" Jim asked jokingly.

"Ha! Never, oh wise one!" Sarah mocked.

"See, that's what a man needs, a woman who sees his wisdom." Jim put his arm around Sarah and squeezed gently.

"Sure. That's what I was doing." She took another drink of her water, and they headed toward the living room to catch some tele-vision. "Let's go see what's on before you get too full of yourself."

"Lead the way," he replied lovingly.

CHAPTER 55

The day had come. Jim, Sarah, Carissa, Isaac, Annabelle, Connie, Betty, and Eric all arrived at the capitol building, one car behind the other. They parked, and everyone piled out of the vehicles and met in the middle of the parking lot. Carissa was so nervous her hands were shaking. She could barely push herself. Her dad stopped her when they had almost reached the others in the parking lot.

"Carissa, I want you to know that, whatever happens today, we are so proud you are our daughter. We couldn't ask for any more than what you've already accomplished. These babies didn't have a voice, and you gave them one. You did this, and we are so overwhelmed at the young lady you've come to be."

"I love you, Dad," Carissa replied, tears filling her eyes. "Now stop, I'm going to ruin my makeup and look crazy before I talk to these people."

Jim patted Carissa on the back, and they travelled the rest of the parking lot to meet up with the others.

What they saw when they looked toward the building was more than Carissa ever could have imagined. There were people as far as she could see, holding signs that said, "Save the Babies" and "Tell the Truth" and all kinds of other slogans. They were chanting things, and waving their hands in the air. Carissa wasn't even sure she could get to where she needed to be.

"Wow," Annabelle said. "I think we're going to have to help clear the way."

They started up to the building, surrounding Carissa and her chair just so she could get through the crowd. When they reached the door to the building, Isaac bent down to Carissa, kissed her on the cheek, and told her he loved her, then Carissa went in alone to support her bill, her baby. The rest of them waited on the steps, where one woman started to pass around a microphone, so people could tell their stories of spina bifida and the untruths they were told.

"My daughter was born with spina bifida thirty-four years ago. We didn't know about the spina bifida beforehand, but the doctors told us we could still let her go if we wanted to. Today, she's nothing like they said, and I'm glad we didn't listen," one woman said.

"I was born with spina bifida. I'm not a vegetable. Ask my wife," a man said.

"My baby was diagnosed in-utero with spina bifida. Because of false information given to me upon diagnosis..." the young woman paused, tears streaming down her face, "I aborted. I regret it every day. There isn't a day I don't tell my child I'm sorry." She paused for a moment, then went on. "This law has to pass so this never happens to another baby. I miss my baby."

With that, the crowd went silent. There wasn't much to say after that. That one young woman bravely said it all. Small groups broke into prayer, and they stayed that way until Carissa and John exited the front doors of the building.

Someone handed Carissa the microphone. Slowly, with tears in her eyes, she lifted the microphone to her face, and simply said, "We did it."

The crowd erupted. She was getting hugs from all directions. She couldn't tell who was who, and she couldn't find her family, until Isaac burst through the crowd. He hugged and kissed her, and then took the microphone for himself.

"Can I get everyone's attention, please?" he shouted into the mic, but only a few heard him.

"Excuse me, can I get your attention?" he shouted louder, and the crowd quieted. "Carissa is my girlfriend. Over the last few months, I've watched her grow as a woman. I've watched her take on the world. I've watched her save countless lives. And I've realized I never want to be without her," he told the crowd.

Then he turned to face Carissa and his face got serious. "Carissa, I called your dad the other day. We had some things to talk about, man to man, and he gave me his blessing to ask you a question in front of all these people. So, if you're embarrassed, blame him."

Carissa started to shake. Was he really? Was this happening, right here on the capitol building steps?

"Carissa?" Isaac knelt down in front of her and reached into his pocket for a box, flipping it open to reveal a beautiful diamond ring. "Will you marry me?"

"Yes!" she screamed, as he slipped the ring on her finger.

The crowd roared so loudly that Isaac barely heard her answer, but barely was good enough for him. He had his girl, and she had her law.

What could be more perfect?

ABOUT THE AUTHOR

 Misty Boyd was born in August of 1983 with spina bifida, the same birth defect as her main character, Carissa, in her novel, *Carissa's Law*.

Upon her arrival, her parents were told she would not live through the night and, if she did, she would be mentally and physically challenged and dependent on others her entire life. They were told she would never walk, talk or feed herself. She would only sit in her wheelchair and be dependent on them for her every need. Her parents were given the option to withhold feeding and let her die. This option was deemed unacceptable and Misty was medically treated at a different local hospital.

Fast forward 34 years… Misty is happy and healthy. There have been obstacles along the way but she walks, talks and is fully independent, with no significant mental challenges. She is married to a supportive husband, and is an incurable lover of Jesus and hedgehogs.

Misty is a Christian, and her relationship with God is very important to her. She can be found in her home church every Sunday, but only the afternoon service! She likes to sleep in past both early services.

She and her husband, James, have been married for 10 years and together for 19. They own a hedgehog named Meatball who is 6 months old. They have no children.

She enjoys both dancing around her apartment, and singing at the top of her lungs in the car, even if she's not very good at either one!

Her favorite food group is Tex-Mex. She can be won over by a good taco 9 out of 10 times!